Serving the
Children
of the World

W9-ACS-760

Purchased with a grant given by
Carrollton Golden K Kiwanis Club
through the Friends of the Library
Matching Gift Program
2013

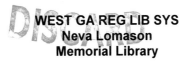

WEST GA REG LIB SYS
Neva Lomason
Memorial Library

young fredle

MORE BOOKS YOU'LL ENJOY

Babe: The Gallant Pig by Dick King-Smith
Fantastic Mr. Fox by Roald Dahl
A Good Horse by Jane Smiley
Hoot by Carl Hiaasen
Rascal: A Dog and His Boy by Ken Wells
Toys Go Out by Emily Jenkins
When Life Gives You O.J. by Erica S. Perl
Where the Red Fern Grows by Wilson Rawls
Whittington by Alan Armstrong

cynthia voigt

young fredle

ILLUSTRATED BY
louise yates

A YEARLING BOOK

Sale of this book without a front cover may be unauthorized. If the book is coverless, it may have been reported to the publisher as "unsold or destroyed" and neither the author nor the publisher may have received payment for it.

This is a work of fiction. Names, characters, places, and incidents either are the product of the author's imagination or are used fictitiously. Any resemblance to actual persons, living or dead, events, or locales is entirely coincidental.

Text copyright © 2011 by Cynthia Voigt
Cover art and interior illustrations copyright © 2011 by Louise Yates

All rights reserved. Published in the United States by Yearling, an imprint of Random House Children's Books, a division of Random House, Inc., New York. Originally published in hardcover in the United States by Alfred A. Knopf, an imprint of Random House Children's Books, New York, in 2011.

Yearling and the jumping horse design are registered trademarks of Random House, Inc.

Visit us on the Web! randomhouse.com/kids

Educators and librarians, for a variety of teaching tools, visit us at randomhouse.com/teachers

The Library of Congress has cataloged the hardcover edition of this work as follows:
Voigt, Cynthia.
Young Fredle / Cynthia Voigt ; with illustrations by Louise Yates. — 1st ed.
p. cm.
Summary: Fredle, a young mouse cast out of his home, faces dangers and predators outside, makes some important discoveries and allies, and learns the meaning of freedom as he struggles to return home.
ISBN 978-0-375-86457-5 (trade) — ISBN 978-0-375-96457-2 (lib. bdg.) —
ISBN 978-0-375-89586-9 (ebook)
[1. Mice—Fiction. 2. Adventure and adventurers—Fiction. 3. Freedom—Fiction. 4. Dogs—Fiction. 5. Cats—Fiction.] I. Yates, Louise, ill. II. Title.
PZ7.V874You 2011
[Fic]—dc22
2010011430

ISBN 978-0-375-85787-4 (pbk.)

Printed in the United States of America

10 9 8 7 6 5 4 3 2 1

First Yearling Edition 2012

Random House Children's Books supports the First Amendment and celebrates the right to read.

For Freddie, of course

contents

1

Between the Walls

"I'm not finished foraging," Fredle protested. There was something on the floor behind the table leg. It didn't smell like food, but you could never be sure. Besides, if it wasn't food, Fredle wondered, what was it?

"That's metal," Axle said, adding, "Mice don't eat metal, Fredle," as if he didn't already know that.

"You're a poet and you don't know it," he snapped back, touching the round, thin disk with his nose. In the dim light of the nighttime kitchen, where all colors were dark, this thing gleamed as silver as the pipes in the cupboard under the sink. It smelled of humans. Fredle wondered what they might use it for, and why its edges were ridged. He wondered about the design on its surface. He'd never seen anything like it—was that a nose sticking out? An eye? And where was the body, if this was a head? He wondered, but he wasn't about to ask his cousin. Sometimes he got tired of knowing less and being bossed around. "*Metal* rhymes with *Fredle*," he explained, to irritate her.

"I'm not waiting around any longer," Axle announced, and she scurried off. Fredle planned to follow, just not right away. He tried licking the metal thing. Cool, and definitely not food. He raised his head and, ears cocked, peered into the darkness.

A mouse could never know what awaited him out in the kitchen. There might be crusts of bread or bits of cookies, chunks of crackers, forgotten carrot ends, or the tasteless thick brown lumps that sometimes rolled up against a wall, behind the stove, or under the humming refrigerator. There were brown things in the cat's bowl, too, if you were hungry enough, if you dared. On the pantry shelf there might be a smear of sweet honey on the side of a glass jar, or a cardboard box of oatmeal or cornflakes to be chewed through, and sometimes it was Cap'n Crunch, which was Fredle's personal favorite, although his mother often warned him that his sweet tooth was going to get him into trouble. In the kitchen there were drops of water clinging to the pipes in the cupboard under the sink, enough to satisfy everybody's thirst. In the kitchen, at night, you never knew what good surprises might be waiting.

However, any mouse out foraging in any kitchen knows to be afraid, and Fredle was no exception. He was out on the open floor under the kitchen table, with only one of its thick legs to hide behind, should the need arise. This flat, round metal thing was worthless, so Fredle moved on. He found a pea to nibble on and swallowed quickly, ears alert for any unmouselike sound, and wondered where Axle had gone off to. He knew better than to stop eating before he was entirely full. If you forage only at night, and always in great danger, you don't stop before you are full enough. Otherwise, you might have to wake early and wait a long, hungry time before the kitchen emptied and the mice could go out, foraging. Fredle would finish the pea before he ran off to find his cousin. He nibbled and chewed.

CRACK!

The kitchen mice froze, and listened. After a few long seconds, they all dashed back to the small hole in one of the pantry doors, shoving and crowding one another to get to a place where the cat—alerted by the sound they all knew was a trap, closing—could not get at them. Only when he was safe on the pantry floor, behind the closed doors, did Fredle step aside and let the rest of the kitchen mice pass him by. He was waiting for Grandfather, who was old and slow. When Grandfather squeezed through the hole, the two of them climbed up between the walls together.

At their nest, the mice counted themselves—"Mother?"

"Grandfather?" "Kortle?" "Kidle?" and on through all fifteen of them—and were breathing a collective sigh of relief when Uncle Dakle came peeping over the rim. "Is she here?" he asked. "Our Axle, is she with your Fredle?"

Went, they all thought, but nobody said it out loud. Right away they started to forget Axle. Fredle, although he knew it was against the rules, silently recalled everything he could about his cousin, the quick sound of her nails on the floorboards, the gleam of her white teeth when she yawned at one of Grandfather's stories, the proud lift of her tail. "Why—" he started to ask, because now he was wondering *why* they had to forget, as if a went mouse had never lived with them, but he was silenced by an odd sound, and there was something he smelled. . . .

Everybody froze, as mice do when they are afraid, waiting motionless and, they hoped, invisible. Everybody listened. Was it a mouse sound they were hearing? It couldn't be a cat, could it? Something was scratching lightly along the floorboards. Was that breathing? What could smell like that? What if the cat had found a way in between the walls?

"Fredle."

The voice was just a thin sound in the darkness, like wood creaking.

"Fredle?"

"Axle!" He scrambled up onto the rim of the nest.

"Stay where you are, Fredle," his mother said. "You don't know—"

But Fredle was already gone. He landed softly on the wide board on which their nests rested.

"Axle," Uncle Dakle asked. "Is that you?"

"Yes but I only want Fredle," came Axle's voice, still weak. "Go home and tell them I'm safe."

When Fredle got to Axle, she was huddled behind one of the thick pieces of wood that rose up into the darkness overhead, backed up against the lath-and-plaster wall. As soon as he got close, he asked, "Is that blood? Is that what blood smells like?"

"Dumb question," Axle said.

Without hesitating, as if he already knew what to do, Fredle started to lick at her wounded right ear. "What happened?" he asked.

"You and your questions," she said. Her voice was still pitched low, almost breathless. "With all this blood, if they see me they'll push me out to went."

Fredle knew she was right. A mouse who was wounded or sick, or too old or too weak to forage, was pushed out onto the pantry floor during the day and left there, never seen again, went. Nobody knew if the humans did it or the cat did it or something else, something unimaginable. They only knew that that was the way of mice, the way that protected their nests from harm and kept the healthy ones safe. He had to lean close to hear Axle say, "I'm pretty sure this will heal."

"Why are you still whispering?" he asked.

Axle didn't answer. She had fainted.

Fredle kept licking until he no longer tasted blood and he could hear Grandfather calling him quietly. "Fredle? Come home, young Fredle."

Home was a wide nest behind the second shelf of the kitchen pantry. Home was made of scraps of soft cotton T-shirts and thick terry-cloth washcloths, woven through with long, cool strips of a silk blouse that, if they hadn't been mice and color-blind to red, they would have known was a cheerful cranberry color, not the dark gray they saw. Their nest was big enough for the whole family, and so comfortable that as soon as you scrambled up over its rim at the end of a long night's foraging, all you wanted to do was curl up and go to sleep. There were two such nests at a distance from one another along this shelf between the pantry wall and the dining room wall, and one or two more could be squeezed in, if necessary. Axle's family had the first one. The nest at the far end, the nest that was wider and softer and safer, tucked way back into a corner, belonged to Fredle's family.

At night their shelf was quiet, but during the day the mice were sometimes disturbed by activity in the kitchen. Sounds were muffled by the walls but loud enough, with thumps and clatterings, with opening and closing of the pantry doors, and with various voices. Whenever he could, Fredle woke up and listened.

Three of the voices belonged to the humans: Mister and Missus, who spoke words, and the baby, who only wailed before falling abruptly silent. Sometimes two more sharp voices, which the mice knew belonged to dogs, barked.

"We're right here! Me and Missus and the baby!" one dog would bark. "Hello, Mister! Hello, Angus!"

"You don't have to step on me," the Angus dog would bark.

At the same time, Missus would be saying, "Hello, lunch is on" or "How did the afternoon go?" and Mister would say, "Settle down, you two. Sit. Good dogs. How's the baby been?" and "An angel," Missus would say, or "A horror."

"Everybody's home!" the Sadie dog would bark.

"Missus is almost always home and the baby stays with her, so you don't have to make such a big deal out of it," the Angus dog would answer impatiently.

"Everybody's home *today*. It's never been today before," Sadie would bark, but more quietly.

The humans and the dogs made noise when they were in the kitchen. The cat, on the other hand, made no sound at all, which was one reason it was so dangerous. The other reasons were its sharp claws and teeth, not to mention its skill at using those weapons to went mice. Moreover, although the humans and the dogs lived somewhere else at night, the cat wandered around in the darkness. As soon as he was old enough to crawl out of the nest, Fredle had been warned about the cat. His grandfather had told him how the cat never tired, never lost patience, could sit motionless for hours with only its long tail moving. The cat pounced, Grandfather said, and a mouse went. Axle said she wasn't afraid of any old cat and she boasted that she would make fun of its long, fat tail and squished-in face, if it ever came her way. This made her parents anxious and Fredle's father cross, while Fredle's mother said she didn't want to hear anything like that from any child of hers. But Fredle thought Axle might just do it and he wished he had been born brave like his cousin.

The night after her misadventure, when they gathered

together at the end of their shelf between the walls before going down to the kitchen, there was Axle, "as fat and sassy as ever," Father grumbled. Fredle was smart enough to wait until everyone had scattered all over the kitchen before joining up with his cousin. She had left a chunk of her right ear behind in the trap. She told Fredle how it happened: "I thought I had the move down. In and out, *whip-whap*, I've done it lots before. That trap was *fast*."

"You were faster," Fredle pointed out.

Father, who had overheard all this, said, "Not fast enough. I hope you've learned your lesson, young Axle. You certainly paid dearly enough for it."

"Who cares about an ear?" asked Fredle, who envied Axle's battle scar.

"You'll see," Father promised, and went off to find Mother, who wanted him to stick close to her and the mouselets when she was foraging.

"There's what's left of a potato chunk over here," Fredle offered. "If you want it."

Axle did, and she bit right into it.

"Do you think humans like having us here to clean up the crumbs?" Fredle asked.

"Well, if it wasn't for us, ants would be all over the kitchen, that's for sure," Axle said.

"But then, why have a cat? Why set traps?"

"You're not asking me to figure out humans, are you, little cousin?"

"But why else would the dogs leave us those brown things to eat?"

"Nobody gives away food," Axle told him. "Even I know that rule."

"And why else—?"

"Sometimes I agree with your parents," Axle said, finishing off the potato. "You ask too many questions and I'm tired of them. Go bother your grandfather."

Grandfather and Fredle often lingered on the pantry floor after the others had scrambled up between the walls. They lingered to talk, and also because Grandfather had grown slow, and he didn't want to hold the others back. Grandfather told Fredle everything he remembered about the long-ago days on the Old Davis Place. "The dogs are new. Not as new as the baby, but I remember when there were no dogs," Grandfather said. "I remember when there were *two* cats, but no traps. Foraging was easier then, without traps."

"Axle can snatch food from traps," Fredle said.

"Your cousin wants to be different."

Fredle knew that, and he admired it.

"It will lead her into trouble," Grandfather warned. "Or worse."

"What's worse?" Fredle wondered.

"I just hope you won't let it lead *you*," Grandfather said. "But we've been talking here too long and your mother will be getting all het up. It's time to get back up home, young Fredle."

At their own nest, Mother *was* awake and worrying. "Where *were* you?"

"You knew we were in the pantry," Grandfather told her as they climbed in over the rim.

"What if Fredle took it into his head to run back into the kitchen? Or followed that cousin of his off somewhere? He's too curious and you can't deny it."

That, Fredle knew, was true. He asked questions and listened to the answers and remembered what he had been told. He enjoyed being curious.

"You know what humans say," his mother said, "and I've heard them saying it with my own ears, especially Missus, and more than once. *Curiosity killed the cat.* Just think about that for one minute, Fredle. Think about what a terrible monster curiosity must be, if it can kill a cat. I don't know about you, but it frightens me just to say the word."

"Now, Mother," Father said in his soothing voice. "You don't have to worry about that right now. Everyone's home safe, so we can sleep."

Fredle was curious about curiosity, and he *did* wonder if mice weren't right to be afraid of it. A couple of nights later, as they waited in the pantry to make the climb back up between the walls, he asked his grandfather, "Do I ask too many questions?"

"Not for me," Grandfather said. "But you don't want to be a bad example to Kidle."

"How could I do that?" asked Fredle.

"By always asking questions. By following Axle around the way you do. By worrying your mother."

"Mother worries about everything, not just me."

Grandfather sighed. He knew.

"She even worries about what's only old stories," Fredle said. "About cellar mice, because they're so rough and rude in the stories. She worries that they're so big and strong, and what if they try to move up into the kitchen? Or attic mice, chewing on paper and cloth up in the cold—what if they start starving and come to take our food? She even worries about outside. Nobody's ever seen outside, nobody even knows if it's really true."

"Does it matter if a story is true?" Grandfather asked.

"Yes!" cried Fredle. "It does! It's hard to understand something if you can't even tell if it's false or true."

"There's only so much a mouse can hope to know, young Fredle," Grandfather advised. "Live longer and you'll learn that. If you're a mouse, you have to accept the way things are."

He was thinking about Grandmother, Fredle knew.

"We all warned her," Grandfather said. "*Bacon*, we told her, *and cheese and peanut butter. That's how humans bait their traps.* Those things might taste good but they lead straight to went. She couldn't have foraged with one leg like that, ruined. We had to push her out, didn't we?"

"What *is* went?" Fredle asked then. Went was the scariest

thing any mouse could do, and the scariest word any mouse spoke or heard, and he had no idea what it was.

Grandfather shook his head. "That's something no mouse has ever known." He sighed again and said, "Time to go on up home."

But Fredle said, "Axle isn't afraid of went. She says so."

"Do I need to remind you that your cousin has only half of a right ear?" asked Grandfather, stern now. "Axle talks foolishness."

Fredle disagreed. "Axle's braver than anyone. Why do mice want all other mice to be so frightened? And all the time?"

"For safety," Grandfather explained. "Without safety, a mouse doesn't have anything. He might as well just run out into the kitchen and went right away and get it over with, because he's bound to went very soon anyway, without safety. *Keep safe* is the number one rule. Your cousin seems to think that rules don't apply to her."

"Do all the rules apply to all the mice all the time?" Fredle wondered. After all, Axle *had* gotten better, despite the terrible wound to her ear. They hadn't had to push *her* out.

"You'll see, I promise you, you'll see. When Axle has a nest of her own and a family of her own, she'll stop all this running about, taking foolish risks, worrying everybody. She'll settle down. So will you, young Fredle, and when that time comes— for which, I can tell you, we will all be very grateful—you two can still go out foraging together, just like you do now, and when you're waiting with your own families by this very same hole for it to be safe to go out into the kitchen, you'll tell stories about all the wild and foolish things Axle did when she was too young to know better. Believe me, young Fredle," Grandfather promised, "both of you will grow up and know better."

And that is probably just what would have happened, had it not been for the Peppermint Pattie.

2

The Peppermint Pattie

It was Fredle who smelled it but it was Axle who led the way up to the highest pantry shelf. They had just emerged onto the pantry floor when Fredle lifted his nose and sniffed. "Smell that? What do you think it is?"

"Let's find out," Axle answered.

And so he followed her back through the pantry wall, keeping close as she climbed, up past the board their nests rested on, digging his nails deep into the soft, prickly insulation so as not to fall. High above the nests, they found an opening that led them through the wall again and out onto a high pantry shelf. There the smell was stronger. It was no surprise that at the very end, behind stacks of bowls and plates, hidden just as Fredle's nest was hidden away, lay the source of the smell.

Fredle had never smelled anything like it before, but anything that smelled like that *had* to be good, better than anything else. It wasn't bacon or cheese or peanut butter, he knew, and it was a thick, flat, round shape, so he was confident that it wasn't a trap.

Axle started right in, chewing through the wrapping, but Fredle walked around it, curious about what it was, enjoying the heavy, sweet smell.

"You could help," Axle complained.

"I found it, didn't I? I'd say that's pretty helpful."

"*I* found it," she corrected, spitting out a mouthful of wrapping. When it was just the two of them, foraging together, they didn't bother about the wrapping rule. Mice were supposed to swallow the wrappings they had to chew through to get to food. As long as mice swallowed the wrappings, the humans wouldn't suspect.

"I *smelled* it, I meant," he said, but he settled down across from his cousin to chew his way into whatever it was that smelled so good, smelled better than anything he had ever smelled before in his whole short life, smelled—somehow, despite the rich sweetness—as fresh and clear as a drop of water.

They got tiny chips of it as they made their way through the inner wrapping. Every now and then, as they chewed and spat, one or the other would stop to ask, "Did you get a taste of that?"

"Just a little bit," the other would answer.

"Wow, I never—"

"Really good."

When Fredle pushed the last bits of paper out of the way with his nose, he breathed in, breathed deep, before he opened his mouth to take a bite. The smell was so strong now, and so alluring, that he didn't even think to call across to Axle to find out if she, too, had made her way through the wrapping. He wanted that taste in his mouth, right now. His teeth crunched through a thin, dark crust to the center, which was what he'd been smelling. With that first bite, his whole mouth filled with sweetness, sugary but more than sugary, entirely smooth and not at all chewy. It had two layers of taste, each wonderful in its own way, and they blended together to make—he took a second bite, then a third—the best taste he had ever had in his mouth.

All Fredle could see of Axle was her ears, one of them rounded and perfect, the other half the size of the first, as if some creature's teeth had taken a big bite out of it—and that was pretty much what had happened, he thought now, bending his own head down to taste that flavor again.

Axle's voice said, "I'm glad you're the one I'm sharing this with, Fredle."

Fredle couldn't resist. "Since I'm the one who discovered it, I'd say *I'm* sharing it with *you*."

"*We* found it, little cousin. We're a team."

For a long time they ate in happy silence, and still there was a wide expanse of the food remaining between them. Fredle's stomach was full but his mouth was not tired of the taste, so he kept on taking little nibbles. Axle came around to sit down heavily beside him.

"Whumph! How can you still be eating?"

"It's so *good*. Do you have any idea what it might be?"

Axle shook her head. "I know it's something I never had before, but that could be a lot of things. Soup, olives . . . there's something called whoopie pie. I've heard the words, but I don't know what they are."

"I bet no mouse ever had this before. If he had, we'd have heard about it." Fredle decided that maybe he *would* take a rest, so they sat together for a while, quiet and contented and excited and pleased with themselves.

Then, "Which of them hid it, and why hide it?" Fredle wondered. "It's definitely hidden, way back here behind these stacks."

"Maybe Missus was hiding it from Mister," Axle suggested.

"Or Mister was hiding it from Missus."

"We can be sure it wasn't the baby." Axle laughed a mouse's squeaking laugh.

"What other words haven't you tasted?" Fredle asked.

"Oh, lots. I forget most of them. Stew and candy bar and

flour, although I think flour might be those white powdery grains that are sometimes left on the floor—you know, the ones that are finer than salt and don't taste as good. There's custard and cocoa, too. I can't remember half of the words I've heard. There's something called kibbles. Don't you wish you could take a taste of something called kibbles?"

"I'm going to have a little more of this," Fredle said. "I've rested long enough. I can fit more in and it tastes . . . I've never even imagined anything that tasted this sweet, whatever it is. Maybe it's kibbles."

"It could be."

"They might come to take it away during the day while we're asleep," Fredle pointed out. "We should eat as much as we possibly can."

So Axle, beside him, began eating again at the kibbles, if that was what it was, and the two of them ate on, until they really could not take another bite. And still, Fredle loved the way that at each new bite his mouth filled up once again with rich, fresh, soft sweetness.

At last, however, he *had* to stop, and he and Axle returned along the pantry shelf to the little hole they had squeezed through. Fredle couldn't make himself scurry fast, even though he knew that until he was back behind the wall he wouldn't be safe, but he tried to hurry, slipping behind stacked plates and glass measuring cups, past piles of spare candles, until at last he saw the hole.

He groaned a little, and that helped him squeeze his swollen stomach through it.

Back behind the wall, before they began their steep

descent, Axle asked, "What do you say we don't tell anyone about it?"

"Why not? There's a lot left. What about Kidle?"

"If anyone knew we'd come up here . . . If anyone knew we were the kind of mice who'd smell something and not be afraid to track it down . . . Think, Fredle. It's bad enough with my ear looking weird. Besides, it's ours. That is, it's ours if whoever put it there doesn't take it away before we come back." She stopped moving, turned around and said to him, "I mean it, Fredle. Promise you won't tell."

"All right," Fredle agreed, but he wasn't happy about it. It was such splendiferous food, his sisters and brothers would be impressed with him for knowing about it. Mother, on the other hand, wouldn't want to risk going so far from home, and up the walls, too, and Father would be suspicious because it was something he'd never had before. Grandfather, however, might just be interested; you could never tell about Grandfather.

Fredle and Axle both felt heavy, stuffed full. "Ouff," Fredle heard himself saying as he followed his cousin. He wasn't used to being so slow, or so clumsy. Axle didn't say anything, but he noticed that she was taking a lot of rests and that her tail dragged as if she didn't have the energy to hold it up in the air. He knew just how she felt. His own tail was dragging.

"Does your head feel heavy?" he asked.

Axle just trudged silently on.

"I mean, mine feels like it's hard to look around, and hard to see and hear. Hard to think."

"Don't talk," Axle said. "Let's just—get home."

Eventually, they did, and although they were late, they

still arrived well before the darkness had faded to light. Axle's was the first nest they came to. There was no sound from beyond the rim except a rumbly snoring. "I don't think I can make it over," Axle whispered to Fredle.

"Of course you can," he whispered back. "You have to, because I don't think I can help push."

"Maybe I'll just sleep here, on the boards," she whispered, lying down with a sigh. "Tired."

Fredle went along to his own nest and found his mother awake and worrying, with Father beside her. "Where have you been?" Father demanded as Fredle struggled to pull his body up and over the rim.

"You're home safe!" his mother cried, but softly, so as not to wake the others.

"Not for long if he goes on like this," Father predicted. "*Now* can I get some sleep, please?"

"I was so *worried*," Mother murmured to Fredle before following Father.

Fredle lay draped over the rim of the nest. He didn't have the energy to apologize or to move, to find his brothers and sisters where they would be piled up warm together, to snuggle up close behind Kidle. He could only stay where he was, with his head propped on the rim, because for some reason, that morning, this was a comfortable position. He felt as if his stomach was fighting with itself.

When Fredle did sleep, it was only the lightest of naps. He dozed and woke up, dozed and woke up, again and again. He couldn't seem to get comfortable, no matter what position he tried, not on his left side, not on his right side, not curled up, not stretched out on his back, not lying on his swollen stomach. He felt bad, maybe sick. But he didn't want to feel bad. It was dangerous to feel bad and especially dangerous to feel sick-bad, so he told himself he was fine.

It was his stomach, no question. What could make his stomach feel so hot, so unhappy? What he had eaten could do that. He knew it perfectly well, but he didn't want to believe that, either. *It'll be better by nightfall*, he told himself. *I'll feel back to normal when I wake up*. That is what he promised himself, half-awake.

If he hadn't been half-awake, or more accurately, if he hadn't been only half-asleep, he wouldn't have heard his name being spoken so softly even his sharp mouse's ears could barely catch it. "Fredle? Fredle?"

He raised his head.

"I can see you. Can you hear me?" It was Axle.

"I don't feel good," Fredle admitted. "Do you?"

"No. That's why—"

"Was it poison? That good thing?" That was Fredle's real fear.

"Do you think so?"

21

Fredle thought. Until then he hadn't really thought about anything at all; he'd just worried and been afraid and tried *not* to think.

"Poison would hurt more," he said. "Probably. Don't you think? Poison is really bad. Strong. And it's quick, I think." Then he remembered something. "*Where there's a cat there won't be poison.* That's one of the rules."

Axle had come up so close that her nose almost touched Fredle's ear, where his head was hanging down over the rim.

"We have to leave," Axle said. "Before they push us out."

Fredle had to tell her, "I can't move." Despite his own words he did try, to find his legs, to lift his head. But his stomach hurt so much that his four legs could only curl up next to it. He wailed, "I can't!"

"Quiet, Fredle. Don't— You have to try harder." Axle's voice grew urgent. "You were groaning. It was loud. How do you think I knew where you were?"

Fredle swallowed back a wail and said again, "I can't move."

"Sometimes, when you can't, you have to anyway," Axle advised him.

Fredle did groan then, keeping it as soft as he could.

"I have to— Goodbye, little cousin, I'm—I'm sorry," Axle

whispered, and before Fredle could say *Please don't go*, she was gone.

Axle was gone and all Fredle could do was whimper, like a newborn mouselet, a little whining sound of sadness and fear. But not hunger. He would never be hungry again and what if his father was awakened by all the noises he was making?

He struggled to be silent, but it was already too late.

3

Outside

They had pushed him out onto the pantry floor and left him there behind its closed doors. He knew he had no chance of getting back behind the wall, even if he had felt well enough to try to fight the mice who would be guarding the hole, or even just argue with them. He had felt too sick to struggle and then he'd been ejected with such force that he was all the way out in the middle of the pantry floor before he came to a halt. Sick and unhappy and frightened, Fredle did what mice do: he froze, and trembled, and waited.

He didn't have to wait long. Maybe if he had had to wait longer he would have gathered himself together and formed some kind of a plan, but almost immediately the pantry door opened and Fredle was blinded by light.

A gasp, above, and the door slammed shut. Now Fredle

could only wait, and now he wondered: What would went be? Whatever could it be, to need a word so huge and dark that nobody wanted to speak it? Did he have to be brave when he met it? And would he always, he wondered miserably, have this pain in his stomach, as if fear had sharp teeth and was chewing its way out from inside him?

He wondered where Axle was now, and if Kidle had already forgotten him. He remembered how he had once invited Kidle to come along with him and Axle, and how his little brother had squeaked so loudly with excitement they had to scold him to be quiet. He wondered why that was what he remembered. He wondered—

The door opened again and Fredle shut his eyes tight against the light and also against having to look at whatever he might see. He heard Mister say in a rumbly voice, too loud and close for Fredle to be able to understand all the words, ". . . Patches will get rid . . ." And Missus's clearer voice said, "I can't just . . ." Mister rumbled something else and Missus said, ". . . a way to take it out . . ."

Fredle kept his eyes closed and his ears open. He thought he should at least try to move, but his hot, heavy stomach weighed him down. He waited, and trembled, and could not think.

With a thump, the air around him closed off and he could no longer hear anything. His eyes flew open then but he could see only a weak, whitened light, gleaming all around him. It was a wall, a round wall. Dim shadows moved behind it. But when he looked down he could still see his two front paws, quite clearly, their gray, bony surfaces and sharp yellow nails, and when he scratched on the pantry floor he could hear a clear *scritch, scritch*.

Looking up, Fredle saw that the pale wall was also close over his head.

Then a new floor slid under the wall, and moved toward him. He backed away. The strange floor scraped over the wood of the pantry floor and Fredle kept backing up until the wall stopped him and he was forced to step onto the sliding floor. It was cool under his feet and hard as glass, but it wasn't glass. It was metal but like glass it was too smooth for his nails to grip, so he slid forward along it until his nose bumped against the opposite wall.

Sliding, thumping, he felt the floor rising up beneath, lifting him. This felt like falling but it was the opposite of falling. Could he fall up? Fredle wondered. As far as he knew, no mouse had ever had this happen to him. Was this went?

Without moving, he was moving; he could feel it. The trap—if this was some new kind of trap—was gliding along smoothly and he could see shadowy shapes moving by, beyond the pale wall. He heard a sound like a door closing, but the movement continued.

Then the floor was falling away and he was falling with it, then stopping, stopping and falling, stopping and falling.

Fredle couldn't catch his breath, for the fear and the feeling sick. Finally the floor swooped down—carrying Fredle with it—until he almost fainted from the speed and steepness of the descent, and then a sudden landing.

What—

The cool, smooth metal floor slipped out from under him, the mysterious trap rose up and disappeared, and he huddled in a light even brighter than the one when the pantry door had opened. This was a light so bright that it hurt to see. He squeezed his eyes shut.

From above him he heard Missus say, "I don't know. I hope you . . ." And then she was gone.

In the darkness of his closed eyes, Fredle felt warm air and he smelled wetness and something else, something entirely strange to him, coming from a floor the likes of which he had never before set his paws on. Keeping his eyes tightly closed, from the brightness and from fear, too, Fredle slid his feet, cautiously, gently, back and forth on this not-floor. It was cooler than wood and not nearly as smooth; also, it was soft. His nails slipped into it. His stomach still felt sick, felt overfull and angry.

Even so, a sharp smell penetrated his senses—a smell of something that made him want to eat it, sick as he was. How could that be? Fredle wondered. How could he possibly think of eating anything? But this was like wanting a drop of the cool water from the pipes under the sink, something different from hunger. He opened his eyes.

Even if he'd never seen anything like them before, Fredle

knew without a doubt that the narrow green strips standing tall all around him were what he was smelling and what he wanted to be eating. Without thinking, he took a bite.

It was stringy and watery and tasteless as a dog's brown chunk. It also took a lot of chewing, but he persevered. He forced it down his throat and waited, to find out how his stomach would react. When he was sure his stomach didn't feel any worse, and because he still wanted more, he ate his way through a whole long stalk of it.

While he was chewing, Fredle looked around. He had to squint against the brightness, but it took so long to make a bite swallowable that he had time to notice lots of things. He noticed how very many of those tall green stalks there were, all around him, and he noticed that straight ahead, hidden behind the stalks, was a dark space, protected by a white wall with holes all over it. He noticed, although without *really* noticing, that he was seeing colors that were bright and clear, not dim and dark. He noticed, too, that his stomach didn't feel as sick as it had, and he went on chewing.

When he'd had enough, Fredle made his way cautiously toward the bright white wall. He pushed his way through the stalks, trying not to let his nails dig into the soft floor, because how could he know that his feet wouldn't sink so deeply into the softness that he'd be trapped? He trod as lightly as he could—and, being a mouse, that was very lightly—until he arrived at a wall with openings all along it as small as mouse-holes, and some of them so low he could easily peer through.

He saw a shadowy light beyond the wall, and the odd floor smell was stronger in there. Nothing moved that he could see or hear, although it wasn't the same kind of empty quiet as a nighttime kitchen. Waiting beyond the white wall there seemed to be a dark, quiet territory, crowded with shadows and smells and sounds too soft and fine even for *his* ears, as if it was inhabited by creatures much smaller even than a mouse.

Most importantly, it smelled and sounded and felt safe, which the green stalks and bright air behind him did not. So Fredle scrambled up through one of the holes and tumbled down into the darkness.

When he landed on a floor even softer than the one he had left behind, he was suddenly exhausted. He was so entirely tired that even being afraid couldn't keep him awake. He dug himself a shallow place close to the white wall and curled himself up in it. It was not until he was about to fall into sleep that he realized: his stomach didn't hurt.

It was noise that woke him. Noise came from over his head and from beyond the wall, thumpings and barkings and behind them a loud roaring that abruptly stopped. But it wasn't silent out there after that. Out there was filled with sounds.

Fredle had sprung awake as suddenly and completely as he had fallen asleep. At first, like any other creature waking up in a new, unknown place, he was confused and alarmed. He didn't know this nest and it wasn't a nest at all. Light was oozing in through the many holes in the wall, there was not as much space over his head as he was used to, and it wasn't warm. He heard only unfamiliar sounds and unfamiliar silences, he saw only an empty space he'd never seen before, and—most odd and unmouselike of all—he was alone.

Beyond the wall, outside, the dogs barked: "Hello, Angus! I took care of the baby!" "We're home! Mister was proud of me!" "Let's run!" Then Mister said, "Hello, you two. Let me hold her for a minute. We took one blue ribbon and two reds. He just keeps improving," and Missus said, "There's a pot roast for supper, are you hungry?" There were loud footsteps over Fredle's head. After that, it was quiet again. Eventually, Fredle grew curious about just exactly what lay beyond his wall. He raised his head high enough to be able to look out through one of the holes and see what there was to see, now that the light wasn't so blindingly bright.

He saw those green stalks, going on and on, but then something above them caught his attention, a dark movement, back and forth. He couldn't make sense of what he saw, until—"Stop, Sadie," one dog panted. "I was working hard all day I'm thirsty." The dogs were *outside*, like he was, Fredle realized. "Let's go in," the dog said, and there were more thumping sounds from above, lighter this time.

After the dogs were gone, Fredle could see that no matter how far he looked up, over the tops of those stalks, he couldn't see a ceiling. The air stretched up and up, and white things floated in it, and it was blue, and pink, too, and a golden orange as well.

Inside, colors were dark and could be seen only rarely, mostly on the boxes and cans on the pantry shelves. Inside, you almost never saw color, but outside, seeing color seemed to be normal. Even the air outside had color, unlike the dim gray air in the nighttime kitchen or in the spaces behind the pantry wall. These tall stalks were green like peas, but brighter. This soft floor was brown, but not nearly as dark as the crust on that good sweet thing.

Remembering, he warned himself not to forget that good sweet thing, because probably that had been what made him sick.

He wanted to remember that because being sick was what had made the mice push him out to went.

Because of which, he continued, thinking it out, Missus had somehow transported him outside and now he was here, alone. With only a white wall full of holes to protect him. With those green stalks crowding up against it. With the air stretching away without a ceiling to end it.

With an empty stomach, too, Fredle realized. But he had no idea where to find food. He could eat those stalks, he knew, but somehow, now, they didn't appeal to him, not the way they had before. They were a kind of food that only tasted right when you were sick, he thought, and then he wondered, Would food that tasted good when you felt bad automatically taste bad when you felt good again?

As he wondered about these things, Fredle was walking along behind the white wall, his nose to the ground, foraging. He foraged without finding anything until his way was blocked by another wall, also made of wood, but without any holes in it. So he turned around and foraged back the way he had come.

He came to the place where he had slept, just a shallow hollow place. He foraged on past it, still following the white wall.

Nothing and nothing and nothing to eat. There was only

the soft floor. He knew that he was going to have to go beyond the white wall again, because now he was getting thirsty, too. At least the bright light had left the air. Fredle felt more comfortable coming out from behind the protection of his wall into darkness, where he could see perfectly well but not himself be easily seen, if there was anything out there to see him.

Was anything alive out there? Fredle hesitated behind his wall, growing more and more frightened. Was there anything waiting out there to went him? A cat, or, worse than a cat? What could it be that was worse than a cat? Then Fredle thought of a new worry. Was there anything to eat out there, and if there was, how would he ever find it? Axle, he knew—and it made him jealous—would just scramble up through one of the holes in the white wall and find out.

Up he scrambled.

On his feet, outside, he hid in among the tall stalks, and listened. The dim air was filled with sounds, none of which he recognized. Moreover, the air outside had changed color and in the distance it now looked a dark gray-blue. What had happened to all that light? But he didn't smell any food and he couldn't tell if the sounds he was hearing—voices? movement? whisperings?—were close or far away.

Fredle felt outside stretching off in front of him. The empty vastness of it made him want to turn and scramble back into his— What was it? You couldn't call it a nest. A nest was lined with soft cloths, it was warm; many mice lived together in a nest. What Fredle had was nothing more than a cradle, but it was still the safest place he knew, and part of him wanted to run back to it.

Except he was so hungry. Fredle gave up and chewed away at one of the stalks, and then he ate another, until his stomach felt full enough. It didn't feel really full, but he was no longer thirsty and he needed to get back behind the wall, to be out of the dangerous outside with all of its strange sounds and all of its emptiness.

Huddled back next to the white wall in the shallow little place that at least smelled familiar, at least smelled like *him*, Fredle wished that Axle had been pushed out with him, and then he wished that he had gone off with her—wherever it was she had gone off to—and then he wished that they had never found that good thing, because that was the beginning of all this badness. Fredle wished and wished and wished, but all the wishing didn't make any difference.

In fact, the wishing made him feel hopeless and hungry and sad, and those feelings mixed in together to make a feeling so bad that he didn't want to be having it. So he went to sleep, even though it wasn't his usual time. He curled up, closed his eyes, and marched himself off, as if sleep were an actual place, like home, like the kitchen—a place a mouse could go to.

4

The Unknown and the Unexpected

For the second time, Fredle was woken up by noise from beyond his white wall, and when he looked out one of the holes he could see that it was daytime again. The air was so bright that Fredle had to blink away tears, to see.

The dark shapes he saw moving against the light made barking sounds, so he could recognize them as the dogs, Angus and Sadie. He hadn't known that dogs were so big, and neither had he realized how very loud their barking was. One of them jumped up out of sight and could be heard running along over Fredle's head (if that was what was happening; that was what it sounded like, anyway), and Fredle was surprised at how a dog's footsteps thumped. Dogs weren't animals that scurried or scuttled, hoping not to be noticed. They weren't afraid of being hunted or caught in a trap. Fredle wondered

34

what it would be like to be a dog, big and loud and free from dangers.

Hiding in the shadows, his nose and eyes looking out through the opening in the wall, Fredle was both frightened and excited. These were dogs up close. There was a bowl set out on the stalks, and when the dogs suddenly appeared, landing in front of him, they both stuck their noses into it and water splashed out.

They must be drinking, Fredle thought. When they'd gone off, he would go out and drink some water himself; some drops had caught on the sides of the stalks, he could see them shining there, and Fredle was, he realized, terribly thirsty.

He was thirsty, hungry, and alone—the three worst things for a mouse to be.

At that thought, fear rose up all over again in Fredle and he would have crept back into his place to escape it in sleep, if it hadn't been for those dogs. Curiosity kept him with nose, ears, and eyes pointed out through the opening.

"I smell mice," said Sadie, lifting her head. Water dropped down off her long tongue and her bright brown ears were cocked toward the wall where Fredle hid and listened. But the dog didn't see Fredle. Fredle was too small,

it was too dark and shadowy behind the wall, and as long as Fredle didn't move he couldn't be seen. He was a mouse; he knew how to freeze.

"Of course you do," answered Angus. "There are mice all over the farm. You know that, Sadie. That's why Mister and Missus have cats."

"But, Angus, this one's different."

"One mouse is no different from any other," Angus announced. His whole head was black, except for his white nose, and his voice had no doubt in it. He sounded just as bossy as Axle and Father, so Fredle's sympathies went immediately to Sadie. "Mice are all the same and none of them are any good to eat, whatever Patches might say."

Patches?

"I like *our* food. Don't you like kibbles?" said Sadie. That made no sense to Fredle and apparently made no sense to Angus, either, because he just snorted and stuck his snout back into the bowl of water. When he'd finished drinking he said, "Let's go check the barn."

"I'll scare those cats, won't I?" Sadie answered as she ran off, out of Fredle's view.

"We'll give those rats something to think about, too," said Angus, following her.

Without further thought, Fredle scrambled out through the hole toward the bowl, to lick at the water dripping off the green stalks next to it. Out of the corner of his eye he thought he saw something sliding by, hidden among the stalks, but when he lifted his head to look he saw nothing but green stalk after green stalk, packed thickly in together, and he went back to licking up water and thinking about the dogs.

The dogs were often in the kitchen; he knew that. Now he knew that they were also outside. He could deduce, therefore, that there was a way to get from the kitchen to outside. And if there was a way to get from the kitchen to outside, there was also a way to get from outside back into the kitchen.

But did you have to be as big and strong as a dog to find it?

Returning to his place, Fredle thought hard. He was thinking so hard about the dogs that he didn't even think to notice that he was no longer blinking in the bright daylight, as if he had gotten used to it, and he almost didn't notice that there, right beside his little nest, was a dried-up piece of orange peel. *Orange peel? What? How did—?* His stomach began to growl and he stopped wondering.

Eating and being full and then falling into a sound sleep, Fredle forgot to think about returning to the kitchen, but he dreamed of home. He dreamed he was back in his round, soft nest, with the warm bodies of his family to curl up next to as he slept.

When he awoke, day still had not ended. The last long lingering rays of light reached in through the holes in his white wall and illuminated the uneven soft floor. For the first time, Fredle could see the wall that marked the opposite side of this territory, so he went over to smell it, and touch it with his nose, and look closely at it. It was rougher, harder, and cooler than his white wooden wall. It was gray and had no holes. In fact, this back wall was made of two different hard things, one of which ran in streaks between the others, sealing off any open spaces, as if to make the whole wall stronger and better at keeping out anything that wanted to get in.

Fredle thought about that and wondered if there might be some crack in this wall, some opening through which a mouse could squeeze his soft bones.

That night, under cover of darkness, Fredle went farther through the tall stalks than he had before, until he came at last to the end of them. At the edge, he peered out into empty black air. Strange sounds filled the darkness, creakings and groanings, chirpings and whistlings, as if that whole nighttime world was busy with life. But nothing moved except for the gently waving stalks. He stood motionless, staring into the night, listening intently. Then he looked up.

"Oh," he breathed. "Oh."

The black air above him was filled with white specks that winked and blinked and trembled. They gave no light. Instead, they sparkled, brightly. Fredle had never seen anything like it before, but it wasn't frightening. It was too beautiful to scare him. His eyes wanted to keep on looking up at all the white brightnesses, to discover if there was any design in them, to see if they moved, to wonder about them.

No mouse had ever said a word that even hinted at such things. Fredle thought that he might be the first mouse ever to see them. That thought made him feel how terribly alone he was, in this unknown outside world, but at the same time excited and glad to be exactly who he was exactly where he was, the first mouse ever to see this.

He lingered there for a long time before at last returning to his place, and when he was woken up the next morning by the same thundering sounds of the dogs jumping down onto the stalks to drink their water and leave drops scattered all around for him, he saw another orange peel beside his bed. Someone had crept silently in during the night and—being careful not to waken Fredle—had left food for him.

Who would be bringing him food? Not a mouse, because mice didn't give food away. And why would food be brought to him? Missus? She knew he was out here because she had carried him out. But Missus was human and humans didn't feed mice, they set traps and had cats to went them. Of course Fredle ate the peel, but still, he wondered. When he had eaten and made a quick run outside to drink the water the dogs left, he returned to his place. For a long time he pretended to sleep. He was waiting, hoping to catch sight of whatever it was that was bringing him food. Then, pretending no longer, he did fall asleep.

An explosion of sound, a deafening noise, woke him. It was just outside his flimsy white wall. He froze, standing stiff-legged on all four paws.

Something came up close, to attack his white wall. It was like a cat closing in on its prey, but no cat was that loud; also, cats didn't approach and then back off to approach again, roaring all the while.

If it was speaking, he couldn't make out any words. Fredle didn't know if he could have even *heard* words, it was so loud and he was so frightened. The whole little space he was trying to call his home roared and echoed, and he ran back to crouch against the cold rear wall, making himself as small as he could.

Suddenly, it stopped.

There was only silence, although the silence rang with the memory of the roaring sound. Then Fredle heard clanking sounds, then Mister talking and the dogs, Sadie's bark quicker and sharper than Angus's. She was saying, "Yes! Run!" and Angus was saying, "Not so fast, stay behind me."

Hearing familiar dog voices soothed Fredle, so, more than a little fearfully, he made his way up to the white wall—ready to bolt back if he needed to. If outside had such horrible monsters living in it, he wasn't sure he should ever go out from behind his wall again. Even with those night brightnesses being so beautiful out there, outside could never feel safe with that kind of noise in it.

Fredle almost didn't dare to lift his nose up and through the hole, and when he did he was sorry he had. Everything was different. Everything had changed. Everything was ruined. All the stalks were lying flat, cut off, never to stand upright again, and the air was filled with their scent. Fredle drew back to his place, and did not know. All he could think was, it couldn't be good.

Because he was watching so warily, he saw the shadow moving across the openings. Once again, fear conquered him. He froze in watchful terror as the shadow filled up one opening and then thrust itself in.

"I bet you're glad to see me," it said, in a voice that was almost familiar.

It was a mouse.

5

Bardo

Fredle's legs gave way beneath him and he sank down onto the soft floor.

"You're frightened," the other mouse remarked, amused, and that irritated Fredle, so he stood up, tail high. "Wouldn't you be?"

"Not if I was you," the mouse said. "If I was a fat, strong house mouse like you? I wouldn't be afraid of anything. Especially not of me."

Now that Fredle had calmed down a little, he noticed that this *was* the scrawniest mouse he'd ever seen, and that the little brown fellow had an orange peel under his front paws. Fredle relaxed. "Are you the one who's been bringing me food?"

"I sure am. You house mice don't know anything about

finding food, so I'm helping you out, since winter's over and starvation isn't a problem for the rest of us."

"Then thanks," Fredle said. "Except for that I just had those stalks for—"

"Stalks?"

"The ones just outside the wall. The wall you came through."

"That's a lattice, not a wall."

"Oh. A lattice. OK," Fredle said. "Just past the lattice, then, there used to be stalks but now they've all been cut down and—"

"Grass," said the little mouse. "It's grass. You have to be pretty desperate to eat grass."

"I was sick."

"You know? I've seen dogs do that. Eat grass. And I've

heard it said—but everybody says it's one of those old stories, you know—that when dogs eat grass something's wrong with them."

"I think it made me feel better," Fredle said.

"Name's Bardo," said the other mouse. "What's your handle?"

"Handle?"

"What you go by? What they call you and you answer? Your *name*."

"Oh. Fredle."

This was a strange encounter and Fredle felt that he didn't understand what was going on. All he could do about it, however, was learn new words. "What's winter?" he asked.

"Winter's cold, there's snow covering the ground. It's almost impossible to forage in winter, besides the usual dangers like the cats, or some raptor."

"Raptor? What's a raptor?"

"A bird of prey," Bardo answered, with a long, patient sigh. "You know, owls or hawks, eagles. You know what a bird is?"

Fredle didn't say anything.

Bardo sighed again. "Birds." He thought. "Birds are covered in feathers—but you probably don't know what a feather is."

Fredle didn't.

"Feathers," Bardo said. "Feathers cover birds, like our fur covers us. It's like if we had blades of grass all over our bodies."

That sounded impossible to Fredle, but he didn't say so.

Bardo went back to take a quick look out through the lattice wall. Peering out, he said, "Birds have two legs, like the

humans, but they don't just go along the ground. They mostly go up into the air."

"They jump?"

Bardo was shaking his head as he turned around to come back to where Fredle stood.

"No, birds have wings, long, flat, broad things, one going out at each— I'll show you, there's always some crow around, a crow's your typical bird. The point is that birds fly through the air, which means they can come at you out of the air, down from the sky. The raptors have long talons for catching mice." He turned to face Fredle and held up his paws, showing his sharp nails.

Fredle didn't need to ask him about talons. He could imagine.

"And they screech." Bardo waited. There was a long silence as they stared at one another. Then, "That nest of yours," Bardo said. "It's just a hole in the ground."

"You mean, in the floor?"

"I mean in the ground, soil, dirt. I thought you house mice liked things comfortable, but you haven't even lined that hole in the ground with grass."

"So what if I like things comfortable?"

"I'm just telling you you'd better bring in some grass before it dries out in the sun and gets stiff, or gets rained on and starts to rot. That's my advice. Or you *could* hightail it back up the steps to the porch, ha-ha."

There were so many new words, Fredle didn't even know

which ones were important to ask the meanings of. "Porch? Steps? Sun?"

"Don't you know anything?" Bardo laughed. "The porch is what you came down from, down the steps. I saw. Missus was carrying you."

"I didn't see *you*. Where were you?"

"I happened to be in the area. I'll tell you, Fredle, I didn't have much hope for you. I've never seen a mouse look so gray."

"All house mice are gray," Fredle told him. Now he went over to an opening. What had Bardo been looking for, or looking at, out there?

"I know that, but you looked grayer."

"Are all of you field mice that brown color?"

"If we weren't, we'd be easy pickings at night," Bardo told him.

Finally there was something Fredle knew about. "But night's the safe time for foraging," he explained.

"You're talking about inside, where the living is easy," Bardo answered. He was a restless creature, uneasy, and he had begun pacing back and forth between the lattice and Fredle. "You don't know anything about real life, you house mice. Food is left out for you, inside, all you have to do is pick it up and eat. I've heard the stories. I know."

"There *is* a cat," Fredle pointed out.

"An indoor cat," said Bardo, scornfully. "Until you've gone up against the barn cats, you don't know anything about how bad a cat can be. Those barn cats take on *rats*."

Fredle had heard about rats, which were giant mice, smart and strong, with a reputation for being vicious.

"Field mice are entirely different from you house mice," Bardo said. "That's why we're different colors, to show how different we are."

Fredle had always thought a mouse was a mouse, and that all mice were pretty much alike. In his experience, all mice needed food and a home and the company of other mice. Now he wondered if Bardo knew something he didn't. He went up close to the field mouse to ask, "In what ways? How are we different?"

They were talking nose to nose, while around them the light faded. "I have to go," Bardo announced. "I'll come back and I'll bring more food when I do, so you stay right here. I'm your go-between."

"Go-between between me and who?" Fredle asked, to delay the time when he would be alone again. "Between me and what?"

Bardo was already out beyond the lattice, but he stuck his head back through the opening to advise Fredle, "You should go get yourself some of that new-cut grass. It'll make a softer nest than dirt." And he was gone.

Fredle took a thoughtful bite of the orange peel, chewed at it, swallowed, and took another bite. He decided to take Bardo's advice about bringing in some grass. It would be hard work, but it would be good to have a soft place to sleep; it would almost be a nest, it would be almost like home. First he would eat, then he'd go out through the lattice, waiting until the air was dark and those bright things would shine, and be beautiful to see.

Those bright things being beautiful made Fredle feel less lonely. Not being hungry helped, too.

* * *

The next time Bardo appeared, it was day. "Rise and shine," Bardo said, his nose right up against Fredle's ear. "Rise and forage."

Fredle startled awake. "What? Who? Bardo?"

"Accustomed to a long day of unbroken slumber, are we? You'll learn better. You're outside now, Fredle."

"What do you want?"

Bardo hadn't brought the promised food, and besides, Fredle wasn't hungry. He was sleepy.

"I'm the go-between, remember? It's my job to show you how to survive outside, although—frankly?—not many house mice can do that. In fact, there's never been one that did, but I like to think there's always a chance."

It took Fredle a minute to think to ask, "Have there been others? Other house mice, I mean."

"The cats drop one every now and then, and if it's not too cut up it can sometimes make it to shelter. But that happens in summer and those mice don't last long, in any case. You're a little earlier than the others and you didn't get here by cat, so who knows? You might be up to it."

"None of them just—somehow—came out of the house?" Fredle asked. Bardo shook his head. "And what's summer?"

"Summer's warm weather, the opposite of winter. I'm here to give you a tour of the farm," Bardo said. He looked into the shadows as if expecting to find out hidden things, his paws moved on the ground as if ready to start running, and the end of his long tail twitched. "Stay close and keep quiet or I can't answer for your safety."

"Shouldn't we wait for night?"

Bardo gave his short, sharp, sarcastic laugh. "Ha-ha. You house mice just don't know, do you? Out here, night's as dangerous as day. Owls," he said, "foxes, and never forget those cats. All of them are out at night. Hunting." He turned back to the lattice wall, scrambled up and through, then stuck his head back in to add, "Not to mention the raccoons. They're the worst of all, real omnivores. You coming?"

Fear made Fredle want to say No. Curiosity made him want to say Yes.

"Or not?" asked Bardo.

"Yes," Fredle decided, but he didn't move.

"I don't have all day," Bardo said.

So Fredle scrambled out into daylight. He blinked as fast as he could, because even though it wasn't as bright as before, when he first stood out in it, daylight still hurt his eyes.

"You'll get used to it," Bardo told him. "Keep looking down at the ground until you do. Lucky for you it's cloudy today."

Fredle, sticking close behind his guide, didn't know what *cloudy* meant, but he wasn't about to ask. He was tired of asking questions, as if he didn't know anything and Bardo knew everything.

They crept along beside the lattice wall, and it was a good thing they hadn't come to the end of it when they heard a stamping, just ahead of and above them. "Back! Back inside!" Bardo ordered as he scrambled up through an opening, and Fredle followed. They huddled close up against the back wall and listened.

The stomping ceased and they heard Missus. "Have a

drink of water. Then I want you two to burn off some of that energy. Run around, wrestle, chase cats, whatever. If it starts to rain, I'll let you back in, I promise."

At the splashing and slurping, Fredle whispered, "Only the dogs."

Bardo shook his head, impatient. "Be quiet!" he hissed.

Fredle shook his head right back at Bardo, and whispered, *"You don't know dogs. They don't eat mice."* He crossed to the lattice wall. Bardo either didn't understand or decided to pay no attention. He neither moved nor spoke. The two mice both kept very quiet and listened carefully, one huddled up against the farthest wall in case of danger, the other close to the lattice, so as not to miss anything.

The dogs were large, clumsy creatures, spilling water all around as they drank out of the same large bowl. When he had drunk his fill, Angus decided, "We'd better check on the chickens, in case of foxes. Or raccoons—those raccoons like to come in close. Or weasels. We better smell around the chicken pen for anything suspicious."

"Do you smell mouse?"

"Not again, Sadie. How about you stop with all this mouse-smelling?"

"This is a different mouse. This is a mouse under the porch."

"All mice smell the same."

Sadie wasn't listening. She came snuffling up to the lattice wall. At the approach of her large black snout, Fredle froze. With her dog's sharp ears, Sadie might hear him moving. Were a dog's sharp ears sharp enough to hear even the almost soundless brush of mouse paws on soft ground? Fredle wondered.

The snout blocked a whole opening, and blocked out much of the light, too. It snuffled, sniffing. "Someone's there."

Fredle didn't move. Bardo didn't move.

"I can smell you."

The mice were silent.

Sadie said, "I *can* smell you," in case she hadn't been heard the first time. She waited some more, snuffled some more, and then asked, "Who's there?" She waited and waited.

Fredle finally answered her, in a faint, whispery voice, as small as an ant's, "Nobody."

"Oh," Sadie said, disappointed. "But I thought—" Then the snout was gone and the empty opening once again filled with light.

The two mice waited for a long time, silent, patient, the way mice do, making sure that all danger has passed. At last, Bardo broke the silence. "That was pretty stupid."

"It worked, didn't it?"

"She'll figure it out before long."

"Then we'd better get going," Fredle announced. This time, *he* led the way out through the lattice wall. Once outside, however, his confidence left him and he let Bardo re-take the lead.

Keeping close to whatever wall was there, the lattice first and then a solid green wall that turned two sharp corners, they came to another lattice, a duplicate of Fredle's. "Those were steps back there," Bardo told Fredle. "Humans use those steps for going into and out of the house, and so do the dogs. And the house cat does, too, sometimes. You never know when the house cat might show up."

This lattice wall, like his own, had stalks of cut grass spread out in front of it. "Is this where you have your nest?" Fredle asked.

"What would our nest be good for here? No, our nest is way far away. You don't know but it's a dangerous trip I take to come find you. It's dangerous everywhere out here so do me a favor and get moving, Fredle. Maybe inside things are different, but outside we don't hang around out in the open." Bardo hurried on ahead. "You have to know where the compost is if you don't want to starve. Because I certainly don't plan to spend the rest of my life bringing you food."

Fredle ran after him.

When they arrived at the end of that second section of lattice wall, Bardo crouched up against a huge, high, green plastic container. "These hold trash," he told Fredle. "There are two of them, impossible to chew through—although sometimes the raccoons knock them over, they know how to do that, they're raccoons—and some food's left for us. But garbage cans make good cover. Knowing where there's good cover is important, outside."

"Inside, too," Fredle told him. Bardo might think that house mice had it easy, but Fredle knew better.

Bardo stared across more cut grass, ears cocked forward. "The barn cats, in daytime—" he said, but didn't finish that thought. "Although daytime is safer than nighttime out here," he advised Fredle, without taking his watchful gaze from what lay ahead. "Looks like rain," he said mysteriously.

Fredle also looked around. The grass lay like a floor, green, drying to pale brown. In the distance before him a different kind of lattice wall rose up, shiny thin lines of wall with tall, thick posts every now and then along its length; Fredle could see right through this wall to brown soil where little green things stood in rows. The air hung heavy and gray above everything. There were no white streaks across it, there was no sun shining even though it wasn't night, there was no blue ceiling. Bardo glanced up briefly and said, warningly, "Clouds covering the sky, and it smells like rain coming. Let's get going."

Sky, Fredle noted to himself. *Clouds*.

"Head for that fence, Fredle. This is the real dangerous part of the trip. Although, you're so much bigger and fatter than I am, I'm not too worried. If one of the barn cats is out hunting, he'll go for you."

Before Fredle could take in what he was being told, Bardo had dashed off into the cut grass and was running away.

Fredle ran after him, across the grass and then over a wide strip of dirt—rough terrain, where he stumbled and scrambled down and then up over the rises—to more cut grass until finally they came to a halt, breathless, behind one of the posts.

"Cover," panted Bardo. "There are posts all along this fence. They make good cover."

Once he'd caught his breath, Fredle asked, "Is that compost behind the fence?"

Bardo shook his head. "It's the garden. You know, vegetables?" He didn't even give Fredle a chance to say *Of course I know vegetables* before he went on, "Beans, peppers, tomatoes, lettuces—sometimes if you dig you find a potato. Potatoes are the best. Or carrots, carrots are good, too, you have to dig for carrots, too. Missus comes here, in the daytime, and so do the barn cats, sometimes, so it's not good for foraging."

Then how did Bardo know so much about it? Fredle wondered, but what he asked was, "What about at night?" He asked that even though he wasn't sure he'd dare to make the long journey at night, if there would be owls coming out of the air at him as well as ground-level hunters.

"Raccoons," Bardo answered. His voice grew serious and his feet shifted uneasily, as if just saying that word made him anxious. "No mouse in his right mind gets close to a raccoon. They're wild, unpredictable. Dangerous, the way— You never know what they might do, they might do anything. Keep clear of raccoons, Fredle."

"Where's your nest?" Fredle asked. "Here in the garden?"

"Ha-ha. No, we're woodshed mice. Over that way," Bardo said, without indicating which way he was speaking of. "Past the chicken pen. There's a snake— Snakes live on mice, look out for snakes, Fredle. They're all over that woodshed. You have to know their habits to keep safe from them."

"What are chickens?" asked Fredle.

"Chickens are nothing to do with you. Compost is to do with you. That's if you're still hungry?"

"Then what's compost?" Fredle asked.

Bardo didn't answer. He just turned to scurry along beside the fence, running from the cover of one post after the other, until the fence came to a wide hill that smelled of rotting things and turned off in another direction. Bardo stopped at that corner and announced, "This is compost."

It was brown like dirt, but it wasn't really dirt, and there were green and white and dark gray and orange things scattered around all through it. Compost smelled like food. A black animal—not a mouse, or a cat, or a dog, or a human—was hopping up the side of the compost on two thin legs, poking into it with a sharp snout and saying something in a loud, ugly voice.

"That's a crow," Bardo said. "Remember I told you I'd show you a crow? It's a bird. See the feathers?"

Fredle had no idea if he was seeing feathers or not.

"Watch, I'll show you *fly*."

Bardo screeched, a high, sharp sound as if his back had just been pierced by a cat's claws. The crow grew wider and wider as it spread out two fat flat arms, and then it jumped up into the air and stayed there, stayed up in the air with no ground under its feet. Moving its arms it went up into the air, higher and higher, and then it was out of sight.

"Flying is what birds do instead of running," Bardo told Fredle.

"Oh," said Fredle. "Oh." He'd never even *imagined* anything like this.

"Pay attention to the compost, Fredle," Bardo said now. "Compost is what's important here."

"Do we eat it?" asked Fredle, too amazed by the sight of that bird, that crow, to be irritated by Bardo's bossiness.

"Not exactly," Bardo laughed. "We forage in it. There's always something here, like, an apple peel or core." Bardo stuck his nose into the dirt and pulled out a dark gray, sweet-smelling thing. "Apple peel. Go ahead, take a bite. Just one, and not a big one."

Fredle did. He'd never tasted this before, and it was a little chewy, but it was certainly food. It had a quiet sweetness, too, and he hoped Bardo would offer him another bite.

"Or banana peels or lettuce or—almost anything," Bardo told him. "If you come foraging every day, you'll find all kinds of different things to eat. And now that the weather's getting warm, they'll feed the dogs outside, right by your lattice, so you'll get some kibbles, too, because those dogs are messy eaters."

Fredle was tired of Bardo being the one who knew things, so he didn't ask about kibbles. Besides, he thought he could guess now exactly what it was: the brown things the dogs ate, and the cat, too. He didn't need to ask.

Bardo pointed with his nose to a place farther up the compost. "Look, over there? See it? There's an orange peel. You should go get it."

Fredle went off, and climbed up through the soft dirt to nose out a stiff piece of orange peel and pull it after him back to where he had left Bardo chewing on the apple.

But Bardo was no longer there.

6

Alone

It took a while for Fredle to figure it out—and then he knew: Bardo had run off. Run off *where* Fredle didn't know, but run off *why* he was afraid he could guess. What if Bardo's go-between job was really a keep-away job? Or even a push-out job? When he understood that Bardo had intended to abandon him there on the compost pile, Fredle could only feel the not-all-rightness of everything.

He hunched down just where he was, on the compost pile, in broad daylight, unable to move his feet. Where did he have to go to, anyway, if he *could* find his feet and make them run somewhere? He didn't even want to eat, although he could smell how good that orange peel would taste. It was eating that had gotten him where he was, out here in the open, lost, alone, afraid. It was wanting to eat something because it smelled so good, and also following another mouse's tail, that's what had done it to him. He'd followed Axle and he'd followed Bardo, and look where that had got him. He wished . . . He wished he'd never gone looking for that good thing on the pantry shelf. He wished . . . He wished he could go back to before he smelled it, back to when everything was comfortable and familiar and safe, and he wasn't alone and sick at heart.

How long he huddled unhappily there on the compost, Fredle didn't know or care. He crouched on the moist, dark brown hill, the chunk of orange peel uneaten between his front paws. He kept his eyes tightly closed and his ears flat against his skull, then he let his ears perk up and opened his eyes, so that he first heard and then saw all the space around him, stretching out beside him over the garden, stretching out before him into that broad expanse of cut grass until the house ended it.

There was no place to hide in cut grass.

Fredle thought maybe he should dig himself a little hole in the compost, which was soft enough for a nest. If he had a nest here, the compost would be his territory and he would never have to go out alone into those empty spaces in search of food.

But Bardo said that the raccoons came foraging in the compost at night. Bardo said no mouse in his right mind went anywhere near a raccoon. On the other hand, if Fredle dug himself a little nest in the compost, and if he made it deep enough to hide himself in, and if some other mice came to forage, Fredle could sneak after them to discover where their nest was, and he might then be able to make himself another little nest near to them and at least be close to company. Even if he would still be absolutely alone.

Really, what he needed was to find a way back into the house. If he could just get back inside . . . As he imagined the journey across the kitchen floor and up through the wall, then the surprise of his father and mother, Grandfather, and especially Kidle when he crept over the rim of their nest, Fredle found himself chewing on the orange rind. With food in his stomach, he found his thoughts becoming quieter, more useful, and he decided that the compost pile would *not* be a good place to live. It was too far from the house and too exposed to predators. It was surrounded by open spaces.

As soon as he thought of those spaces, Fredle could feel fear begin to swell up inside of him again, starting in his belly and growing bigger and darker and—

So he made himself think about other things. About what he would ask Bardo, if he ever saw that mouse again. If Bardo ever came back, Fredle wouldn't ask what that mouse had been thinking of, leaving Fredle on the compost pile like that. Instead, he'd ask if there was any way into the house. He'd ask if any other mice lived nearby, and where they were. He would ask Bardo about those lights in the night air, too.

And then, after he had answers to all those questions, he might give Bardo a good snap on the snoot, just to let that faithless field mouse know what he thought of him.

Fredle ate until he was full and then he began the journey back, back past the garden fence and across the strip of uneven dirt, with its ruts to slip down and high ridges to scramble over, back at a run across the cut grass to take shelter and catch his breath behind the garbage cans, back to the first lattice wall and then, this time at a slow creeping pace, all around the steps until—at last—he scrambled through his own lattice wall to the safety of his own little nest. The soft lining of grass that he had put into it welcomed him and he curled up in its comfort. Loneliness was all around him, like the air, but he ignored it as best he could and dropped off into an uneasy sleep.

Fredle was awake. His heart beating fast. It was dark and he didn't know what had jerked him up out of sleep. Then he heard it. What was that?

He lay still and listened. It sounded almost as if hundreds of mice were running back and forth just beyond the lattice wall.

Because it didn't sound *exactly* like mice, he lay for a long time, listening.

All the little noises, each separate but also all mixing together—were ants attacking the house? Did ants know a way inside? That question got Fredle out of his nest and over to one of the openings in the lattice.

He looked out into a black darkness through which silver things were falling, falling down through the air, maybe in long lines, maybe just little silver speckles—Fredle couldn't see them clearly enough to know for sure. What had Bardo said? *Looks like rain.* Bardo had said that when he looked at the gray air, and Fredle thought that these falling things might be rain, falling out of the sky, making little sounds when they hit the ground. Bardo hadn't said rain was dangerous, so Fredle stuck his head out through the lattice.

Wet! It was wet and—he stuck his tongue out and then drew it quickly back into his mouth, tasting—it was water, just like the water on the stalks of grass, just like the drops of water on the pipes under the sink.

Fredle was thirsty, so he spent a while with his head stuck out through an opening, using his tongue to catch the water. Then he pulled his wet head back inside. He was cold now; his ears, especially, felt wet and cold. Inside, at home in his own family nest, Fredle had never been cold. Sometimes, out in the kitchen in the dead of night, he had felt a little chilly, but as soon as he got back behind the pantry wall it was warm, and by the time he scrambled into the nest and curled up next to his brothers and sisters, he couldn't even remember what chilly felt like. Here, outside, it was different. The cold started with his ears and then spread to his paws and his tail, even though they weren't wet. Here, the dirt under his paws grew damp and chilly. Moreover, now that he had reminded himself of home, there was a coldness inside of him, too, growing larger, as if it planned to meet up with the coldness outside and turn Fredle into a total misery.

Just what *had* Bardo been up to, bringing him food but then leaving him out on the compost?

Fredle was alone outside, alone and cold, alone and frightened, alone and hungry. There was nothing he could do about it, he realized, and that realization was colder than even the night rain, more frightening even than went. So frightening—

Fredle ran away from it. He didn't think, he couldn't think, his feet just moved as fast as they could, as if he could

run away from his own ideas. He ran across to the hard back wall and scraped his nose all along it, searching for an opening. There had to be an opening. He'd make one, with his claws. He scratched and scratched against the hard surface, but after a while his paws started to hurt and he hadn't made any progress at all, and he knew he never would. So he ran, again. He ran until he hit a wooden wall and then he ran back along the lattice, hoping to find something, anything, some food, some way back into the house. His mind raced as fast as his feet but he couldn't think, all he could do was feel the loneliness, all around him, filling the air and making it hard to breathe.

Fredle ran until he had to stop, the sound of his own breathing loud in his ears. He had thought he'd pushed the loneliness away, but now it was back, and stronger than before. He couldn't outrun it and he couldn't drive it away. He'd never escape it. He'd never find his way home and what would he eat?

Tears started to flow from his eyes.

Mice don't cry. That was one of the rules Grandfather had taught him and Fredle repeated it to himself. *Mice don't cry.*

Yeah, well, maybe, Fredle answered Grandfather silently. *But mice don't live alone, either, and house mice don't go outside, so so much for those rules.* Also, he couldn't stand being alone like this for one more instant. It was more than he could bear. He wanted to go home. He knew he couldn't and he wanted to and he had never been more miserable in his life.

But now he was also wondering: Was home still the nest behind the pantry wall? Or was home now the little place lined with soft grass where he had been sleeping since he'd arrived outside? How many sleeps did it take to make a home?

With all of these questions in his mind, the loneliness was being pushed back, away into some more distant place and that was—Fredle remarked to himself as he felt his breathing grow more steady—a good thing. A very good thing.

By this time, Fredle had dried off. His little nest was the nearest thing to home he had, for now, and he wasn't really hungry—a lucky thing, since he didn't want to have to go out in all that cold, wet water trying to find something to eat—and he had had plenty to drink. So he curled up to think, but not about himself. Instead, he thought about what Bardo had shown him, and what Bardo had told him, and especially what Bardo hadn't wanted him to notice.

It didn't take Fredle long to begin getting curious about those chickens, and after a while he drifted off to sleep.

When he awoke again, it was daylight and the rain had stopped falling. Looking out through the opening in the lattice, Fredle noted that the daylight now had a golden shine to it. He could see the grass lying flat on the ground and the brown rutted dirt beyond, and beyond that something very large, a big, dark gray, house-shaped building in the distance. Could that be the chicken pen? The woodshed? Bardo had talked about a snake in the woodshed. Keep away from that snake, Bardo had said; that snake lives on mice.

All that talk about how dangerous the snake was and no talk at all about chickens—whatever they were. That was making Fredle very curious indeed.

He was also hungry. And he realized, all this wondering about Bardo, and the chickens, and even the hunger, too—all of these things pushed the sad and solitary feeling farther away. As soon as he'd thought that, Fredle could see loneliness oozing back toward him, ready to make him miserable all over again, so he squeezed himself through an opening, tumbling out into the cool, clear air, and froze, right next to the lattice, to listen, to smell, to look.

He saw nothing that looked dangerous and heard only sounds from afar—a distant rumble, one dog barking two quick sharp barks, somewhere the crying baby. Hoping it was safe, Fredle ran quickly along the route that rounded the steps and went in front of the other lattice wall to the big green garbage cans. To get to the garden fence he was going to have to cross the cut grass and the rutted dirt. He was going to have to go fast, and alone. There was no Bardo to lead him, no Axle to tell him to follow close. He was going to have to do it all by himself.

Then Fredle realized: he was going to *get* to do it all by himself.

His heart grew lighter and he made the run, paws tangling a little in grass that lay flat and thick, bony toes stubbing on the rough dirt, until he came to rest again, close up to the foot of a garden fence post. Then he went on more slowly, to the compost pile nearby, where he found potato peels and a carrot top. When he had eaten enough, he lay on the soft pile and thought about where he wanted to go next.

After foraging, you went home to sleep: that was the way mice did things. But Fredle didn't want to rest; he wanted to learn about the chickens.

Fredle trotted off toward the far corner of the garden fence. When he heard a dog barking—Sadie, by the sound of her— and Missus responding, Fredle froze behind a post. At first he just listened, then he took the chance of peeping around.

Missus was carrying a basket in one hand and a bucket in the other. She and Sadie were heading away from the garden to where another fence rose, behind which things moved and chittered. Fredle guessed that either the basket or the bucket had the baby in it.

"It's such a nice day," Missus said. "We can all use a little sunshine."

"Sunshine, yes!" Sadie barked. "Look out, chickens, here we come! And sunshine, too!" She ran on ahead.

The gabble from behind that high fence grew louder, and Fredle, making a dash up to the next fence post for a better view, saw that there were birds in there, kept prisoners—or were they kept safe?—by the fence.

"Sadie? Down. Stay. I need you to watch the baby," Missus said, and Sadie lay down beside the basket with her nose on her paws, while Missus opened a door in the high fence and went inside.

The birds—

But were they birds? Fredle could see wings flapping as they gathered around Missus's legs, but they weren't flying through the air, so could they be birds? Also, instead of making occasional loud comments like the crows, these birds chuckled and chittered constantly. Then his attention was caught by Missus, who reached into her bucket and threw something out around her, scattering it by the handful. Seeing how the chickens reacted, Fredle guessed it was food she was giving them.

The food sprayed around, in all directions, and the chickens scrabbled around after it, pecking and gabbling. Missus stood and watched this for a few minutes; then she left the fenced area, through the same door.

"Good dog, Sadie," she said. "You're an excellent nanny. That'll do."

Sadie got up. "I smell that mouse," she said, but Missus didn't understand.

"Shall we take a little stroll down to the barn and see

66

what's new with the cows?" Missus asked. "You haven't seen the cows for a few days, Sadie."

"But I did," said Sadie. "Yesterday and before that, too. Angus checks them with me."

"And neither have I," Missus said, and they walked off, Missus carrying both the bucket and the basket.

The baby hadn't made a sound. Fredle guessed that it was asleep, and he wondered if babies slept whenever they felt like it, daytime or nighttime, unlike house mice but very like the way he himself was sleeping now.

The chickens were working busily to fill their stomachs—heads down, sharp yellow noses pecking at the ground. As Fredle watched, they wandered around, even putting a head through the fence every now and then.

Probably, the way Missus tossed the food all around her, some must fall out through the fence, and Fredle wondered what that food was, if it was something a mouse might like. He was, he realized, enjoying himself. It was interesting to see all these new sights, think all these new thoughts, learn about all these new places and the things in them. When you were alone, you didn't have to talk to anybody else, or take care of them, or wonder if you were getting in their way or be cross if they were getting in your way. When you were alone, nothing interfered with you.

Fredle decided to go closer to the chicken pen and find out what that food was, if he could eat it. The chickens were trapped inside their fence, so they couldn't harm him with either their pecking noses or their flapping wings. Chattering away quietly to themselves, the chickens didn't pay attention to anything besides their food, so why shouldn't he satisfy his curiosity? He was about to move out of the shelter of the post when he noticed movement in the grass beyond the chicken pen, little twitches of brown in all the green, so swift and silent that only the sharp eyes of a mouse could catch it, and recognize it.

They were brown field mice and they were running toward the chicken pen, all together, from the direction opposite Fredle's lookout behind the fence post. They had been waiting together for Missus to feed the chickens, just the way a family of house mice gathered behind the hole in the pantry door, waiting to go out into the nighttime kitchen. As Fredle watched them, a dark puddle of bad, jealous, sad feelings rose up inside him.

It was loneliness, the bad feeling. Loneliness was back and worse than ever, with the sight of this family of field mice foraging together. Fredle knew better than to try to go out and join them. They might be scrawny brown field mice but they were still mice. Mice don't share and they don't like strangers and they don't like changes.

Slowly, Fredle returned to his own solitary nest, so unhappy that he didn't even try to be careful to stay under cover or race across open spaces. Loneliness wrapped itself up close and cold around Fredle. What could he do but go to sleep?

When Fredle next awoke, it was night and he was thirsty. For a while, he waited behind his lattice wall, watching and listening for possible danger; then he scrambled through an opening down onto the dark, grassy ground. There, he forgot all about being thirsty, because sharp and bright in the black air those lights were shining again. What they might be, he didn't know, but there they were, hanging in the air, motionless, twinkling. Beautiful.

Somehow, looking up at those brightnesses, Fredle felt less alone. Why should that be? he wondered. He knew perfectly well that he was still one small mouse, far from his family and his own nest, alone outside. He knew there was no other mouse nearby to warn him, to flee from danger beside him, to help him keep safe. Fredle knew all that, but he still felt the loneliness drawing back, until it was as distant as those brightnesses. He breathed in deeply and kept on looking up.

He looked and looked. He couldn't stop looking. They were so strange and lovely, those white, sparkling brightnesses with blackness all around them. He wanted never to stop looking at them, as long as they were there in the air to be seen. He thought that, like loneliness, they were sometimes present and sometimes not.

That thought distracted him, and he stared into the closer darkness. A second ago he had felt happily alone but now he felt sadly alone. Loneliness, he thought, came and went, kept changing. Or maybe it was him that kept changing?

But mice didn't change. They didn't change territory and they didn't change food and they didn't change feelings. Mice stayed the same—same nests, same days asleep, and same nights foraging for the same food. Change made things different and that could be dangerous, so mice didn't tolerate it.

What was Fredle supposed to do about all this changing that was being forced on him?

He guessed that all he *could* do was enjoy the good things and endure the bad things. He guessed that was all any mouse could do. And since the brightnesses were very good things, Fredle stayed where he was, staring up into the dark air, where they glittered and glimmered.

7

Neldo

Fredle spent the next days and nights thinking, wondering, foraging in the compost, and sleeping. Sometimes the brightnesses appeared in the night sky and sometimes they did not. Sometimes a single, much larger brightness floated up among them. As night after night went by, he discovered that there were several of these larger things, in several curving shapes and sizes, even one so large and round and white that its light cast shadows like the sun in daylight.

One daytime he was awakened from a light sleep by a snuffling sound, close by, separated from him only by the thin lattice wall. He froze in his nest.

"I smell you."

It was Sadie's voice.

"I'm a good smeller. I'm the nanny and if there's one of

those lights moving around on the floor I'm the dancing dog. What are you?"

Fredle stayed still, stayed silent.

"I know you're under there. I think you're a mouse."

Fredle didn't move.

"I'm just a dog," Sadie said. She waited. "Can't you hear me? You're living under the porch, aren't you."

"No," whispered Fredle, as softly as he could so as not to sound at all like a mouse.

"Oh." She sounded disappointed. "I thought . . ." She must have turned her head away because Fredle had to strain his ears to hear what she said next. "You're right, there's no one there."

"I told you," Angus answered.

"He said so," Sadie said, and the dogs ran off.

Fredle remained in his nest for a time, alert, watchful. He was waiting for the light outside to increase a little, but not too much. That was the time he had decided was safest for the long journey to the compost pile. Whispering voices distracted him from his thoughts—and they were whispering mouse voices! He perked up his ears to catch what they were saying and made himself stay still, despite his excitement.

"I *said*, go away," said an irritated voice that Fredle recognized as Bardo's. The voice that answered he did not know.

"Won't."

"You followed me."

"So what?"

"You know the rules. Only the go-between is allowed. You better go home, Neldo."

"You can't make me."

82

There were two of them, quarreling in angry whispers just beyond the lattice.

"You don't know these house mice."

"He's just a mouse."

"He's bigger than us, and stronger, and *gray*."

"I'm not afraid. I'm not afraid of him and I'm not afraid of you, either, so don't bother showing me your teeth, Bardo. You don't scare me."

"Then I'll tell Father and *he'll* make you afraid. Believe me, if you don't go home right now I'm telling him."

"Just let me look. Just one peek?"

"Then you'll go?"

"I promise."

Fredle relaxed his ears, closed his eyes and breathed slowly, in and out, in and out. He waited. He heard soft sounds from beyond the lattice and then Bardo said, "You promised," and everything was quiet again.

It stayed quiet for a long time, until finally Fredle heard just the smallest sound, as if tiny claws were scratching lightly for a hold on one of the openings. This was followed by the softest of thumps, as a mouse landed behind the lattice wall. Fredle sprang up, eyes wide open, and got himself between Bardo and escape before that scrawny little mouse even knew what was happening.

Bardo dropped the orange peel he'd been carrying in his mouth. His eyes looked from side to side, to see where he might run, but when he spoke it was in a normal and friendly voice that Fredle didn't trust for one minute. "Hey, Fredle. You're awake."

Fredle didn't say anything. He waited, to hear what lies and half-truths Bardo would try out on him. He had figured out, during all the long, lonely nights and days, that if he looked carefully at the untrue things Bardo said, he could catch glimpses of the true things Bardo was trying to hide.

"So," said Bardo. "In that case"—he pushed the orange peel toward Fredle—"this is for you." Then he waited, paws moving restlessly. When Fredle neither moved nor spoke, Bardo said, "Don't you say thanks to the someone who's been bringing you food whenever he can? Getting himself in trouble for it?"

"What do you mean *trouble*?" asked Fredle, not even trying to sound friendly.

"Everybody-angry-at-you trouble."

"You're the go-between. It's your job."

"You don't know anything about anything, Fredle," Bardo told him and Fredle guessed that here, outside, that was pretty true.

"What do you say we go out for a forage?" Bardo asked.

"Sure. OK." Fredle had a lot more questions he wanted to ask.

"What about this peel I brought you?"

"You can keep it," Fredle said.

"What *is* garbage, anyway?" he asked Bardo when they had come to a safe shelter behind one of the large green containers.

"Stuff that's too heavy to carry all the way to the compost," he answered, in the confident way that made Fredle suspect that he didn't know.

"Like what?" Fredle asked.

"Are you trying to irritate me?" Bardo demanded. "Because you're starting to, with all these questions. Just pay attention to not getting eaten, Fredle. Think you can manage that?"

Instead of quarreling, Fredle asked about the brightnesses in the sky. Bardo told him that the humans called the tiny ones stars. "I heard Mister, it was a winter night and he said it to Missus, *Look at those stars*. Then she called one of the big ones—"

"I've seen those, too," Fredle said. *Stars*, he repeated silently to himself, for the pleasure of saying the word. *Stars*. Just saying it made him remember, as if he could see them now, those white twinkling things.

Bardo ignored him. "—moon, she called it a moon. Moons don't look at all the same as stars and no mouse knows exactly how many of them there are. And the biggest one? It's almost as bright as the sun."

"I know," Fredle said.

"And don't dawdle on the road," Bardo told him as they scrambled across the rough dirt strip.

Road, Fredle repeated to himself.

"One of those machines can run right over you on the road," Bardo warned him. "Squoosh you flat. Went you before you know it."

At the compost, Fredle chewed some green, leafy food (celery, or lettuce, maybe chard—Bardo admitted that he didn't know for sure, and *that* Fredle did believe) while continuing to ask questions about the names of things. Only once did Bardo mention chickens ("You never get chicken or any meat or bones in the compost"), but he was happy to talk about the snakes in the woodshed ("Black, they're black and real long"). Bardo reminded Fredle that the snakes were dangerous. "You don't want to get anywhere close to those snakes, or that woodshed. They're worse than any owl or raccoon."

Owls, Fredle knew by then, were birds that hunted by night, swooping down out of the sky to seize mice in their sharp talons and fly off with them. Raccoons, however, sounded more like dogs to him, and he knew that dogs didn't hunt mice. "What's so bad about raccoons?" he asked.

Bardo was glad to tell him. "There's nothing worse than a raccoon, and they run in packs, a lot of them at once. They're a natural enemy, every mouse knows that. They get into everything, hunt by night, take whatever they want out of the garden—there's nothing good about a raccoon. Dirty, quarrelsome, untrustworthy. Mice steer clear of them. There's nothing they won't eat. Chickens, mice, lettuce—rats, too, for all I know. The barn cats don't dare bother them. I *have* heard that the dogs can chase them off, but I've never seen it, myself."

"I don't see what's so bad about all that," Fredle insisted.

"What does a house mouse know except how to lie around and get fat? That's why you have a go-between," Bardo reminded him.

"Hunh," Fredle answered, and they parted company at the garden gate.

"I'll watch you safe back to the garbage cans," Bardo offered, as if he cared about the house mouse's safety.

Fredle thanked him, but he knew better; he could see the

chicken pen and what must be the woodshed beyond. However, since he didn't want Bardo to know how much he knew, Fredle scurried off across the grass.

When he entered the dim light of his own territory, he knew immediately that something wasn't right. He wondered: Who? What? Was he in danger? Pretending to have sensed nothing odd, he listened to the faint, eager breathing and located his visitor, over in a corner where the lattice wall met the steps. Fredle positioned himself with his back to the hard, solid rear wall. He was pretty sure it was another mouse. What would another mouse want with him? Was he in danger?

Fredle had never fought. Mice didn't fight. Of course, he had wrestled around with his brothers and sisters the way mouselets always do, but that wasn't real. But if this was some stranger up to no good, Fredle was ready for a fight.

He jumped up, without warning, leapt from his position by the wall to land on all four feet facing the visitor. Then he walked slowly—threateningly—toward the other mouse.

It said, "How did you know I was here?" and wasn't a bit afraid.

He thought he recognized the voice and decided to surprise her. "Hello, Neldo."

"How do you— Bardo told you about me, didn't he? What did he tell you about me?" She came up closer to Fredle, a field mouse even smaller and scrawnier than her brother, but just as brown. "It's probably true what he said, but not the way he makes it sound. I make them nervous," she explained, and then fell silent, staring at Fredle.

Before Fredle could say anything, however, before he could

ask her what she was doing there, why she made them nervous, whoever *they* were, or what she wanted with him, she asked, "What's your name? Bardo doesn't tell us names. He's the go-between, did he tell you?"

Fredle nodded.

"I don't know why they call him that, since his job is to keep you away from us. What *is* your name?"

"Fredle."

That seemed to please her. "Fredle," she repeated. "He said you were a giant, almost as big as a rat. But Bardo's a liar, sometimes."

"I've noticed," Fredle said.

"Most of it's just mischief, although—sometimes?—it's pretty mean mischief. You can never be sure about Bardo. *I* think they should let *me* be go-between, but they don't trust me to do what I'm told. They think I don't care about the rules. They're right, but I'd still make a better go-between."

Like her brother, she talked a lot. In fact, she was a chatterer, and Fredle began to hope she might be willing to tell him a way back into the house, a way home.

"He says you're nasty. Are you?"

"No," Fredle said.

"I bet you don't bite, either, do you."

"Only food, so far in my life," Fredle said.

"But how did you escape? From inside the house, I mean, because they keep the inside mice like chickens, that's what I've heard. Was it scary, escaping?"

Neldo had mixed everything up. "Why would they keep us like chickens?" he asked.

"To eat. Everything eats mice," she explained. "We're at the bottom of the food chain, except maybe for ants. And beetles. And spiders, too. Not counting vegetables, of course, especially the vegetables that grow out in the open, the tomatoes and peppers, lettuce and beans? They're the real bottom because they're so easy to forage."

"But aren't all vegetables the same?" Fredle asked.

Neldo gave the little squeaking sound that is a mouse's laugh, and rarely heard. "That's like saying all mice are the same and just look at us two, a field mouse and a house mouse, look how different we are."

"There *is* something to what you say," Fredle said. He guessed that if he could change his sleeping and eating habits, he could change his opinions, too. "And the differences don't end with looks, do they? I'm a kitchen house mouse, which is different from being a cellar house mouse or an attic house mouse."

"I'm a woodshed field mouse," Neldo announced.

Fredle asked, "Aren't there snakes in the woodshed?"

"There's only one I ever heard of. It's not easy, being a woodshed mouse, even though, actually, the snake lives up in the rafters and our nest is way at the back, in the bottom layer of wood." Then she changed the subject. "Bardo says you're easy to fool. Are you?"

"I don't know," Fredle said. "Maybe." He thought about it. "But maybe not."

"I think that if you escaped from the house you must be something special," Neldo decided.

This was a compliment Fredle didn't deserve. "I didn't escape. No house mouse wants to go outside. It's not as if we're prisoners, inside. We live there."

"Then what are you doing out here?" she asked.

"Well," he said, starting at the beginning of the story, with finding the good thing.

Neldo interrupted him almost immediately. "It was brown? It was sweet? Don't you know what that is?"

"The inside was white and it was almost all inside. The brown was only a thin shell. That white soft filling was . . . It tasted"—and unexpectedly Fredle could remember exactly how that flavor spread out in his mouth— "wonderful."

"Chocolate, that was chocolate, that shell, I bet. We *never* eat chocolate," Neldo told him, sounding a little bossy now. "Chocolate's bad for mice."

"How was I supposed to know that?"

"You're a mouse. Where are your survival instincts?"

"I don't know how you can talk to me about survival instincts when you live with a snake."

They had made one another cross, and sat silent for a while, until Neldo asked, "Aren't you going to finish the story? About how you escaped?"

"If I have to," Fredle answered grumpily, and so he did, which, strangely, cheered him up.

When he'd finished, Neldo remarked, "Missus saved your life. Do you think she meant to?"

"Why would she want to do that?"

"Nobody saves mice," Neldo agreed. "In the woodshed, if you're too old, you're left—we push that mouse out, we have to. Or if he's sick? That mouse gets pushed out into the open space in front of the woodpile. For the snake."

Then Neldo stopped talking.

Fredle told her, "When we push ours out, they just disappear. I think, maybe, the cat?"

"If there's a cat in the house there's no maybe about it."

"I guess every mouse has to went, sooner or later," Fredle said, sounding to his own ears a lot like Grandfather. "It's the rule."

"I'm hoping for later," Neldo said. "*Much* later. What do you think happened to Axle? I bet she'd like me."

Fredle shook his head; he had no idea what might have happened to Axle, although he guessed she hadn't found her way outside. He told Neldo, "I need to find a way back in."

"Why?"

"It's home. It's where my family is."

"I wish you could come live with us," Neldo said, but they both knew that wasn't possible. That was not the way mice did things.

"I wish I could find a way back," Fredle countered.

Neldo thought about that for a while. "We'll find one," she decided.

"I already looked. There wasn't any."

"You've been all the way around to the front of the house?"

"What do you mean, the front of the house?" asked Fredle.

"The house has four sides and this is only one of them, but—Fredle?—I'm hungry. Let's forage," Neldo said, and she jumped up. "They'll start to wonder where I am and come looking and I don't want them to find me here."

8

Around Front

Neldo set right to work helping Fredle look for a way back inside. The next midday, Fredle was at the compost pile taking bites out of an apple core and deciding if there was any way he could dig a hole large enough for a long crust of bread, or if he had to chew it into smaller sections, which would be easier to hide. He had decided to try digging one big hole and was working his paws hard, his nose buried in the soft compost, when he felt something damp and rather cold jabbed into his rib cage.

He froze, nose in the compost.

"What's *wrong* with you, Fredle?"

It was Neldo's voice.

"You're supposed to run. *Run first, look later,* that's the rule, that's the way mice save themselves. Is it different for house mice? But what are you doing, foraging now? Don't you know this is the time Snake and Fox come out from the barn?"

"Snake and Fox?"

"After they have a morning's sleep, after the night's hunting," Neldo said.

"A snake and a fox together?"

"No, of course not. Don't you know anything? I'm talking about Snake the cat, not Snake the snake. And Fox the cat, who isn't a fox, either. Besides, foxes almost never go after mice. They like chickens, and eggs, and rabbits. They like their food bigger, except for eggs. But everything eats eggs, even humans. So maybe it's eggs that are the bottom of the food chain?"

"Bardo said this was the best time."

"Don't blame Bardo. He has to do what's best for his family. It's not as if he *wants* you went. In fact, I think he likes you, or anyway he admires you, or at least he doesn't understand you. Come *on*."

Before Fredle could ask her what she meant by that, she had run off. Fredle followed her along the garden fence, scurrying from post to post, across the rutted dirt road until they were safe behind the garbage cans. Once he'd learned how much danger he'd been in, Fredle had run faster and more nervously than usual, so it took him a minute to catch his breath, but when he did he asked Neldo, "Then what are *you* doing, foraging at midday?"

"I wasn't foraging, I was looking for you. Nobody will notice that I'm gone, not at midday. They're all asleep. I thought we could look around front for your way back into the house. Didn't we plan to look around front?"

"I haven't decided if I want to," Fredle objected. He was feeling overwhelmed, as if he didn't understand anything anymore. That feeling made him want to stay just where he was, until he *did* understand. After all, it *was* true that as well as being more easily seen in the bright midday light you could also see better yourself, which meant that it might be just as safe to forage at midday as at any other time. That would mean that Bardo had given him good advice, although he was fairly sure that Bardo had no intention of helping him. But Bardo *had* helped him, and maybe he had wanted to. How was Fredle supposed to know what was true? Not knowing how to know made him cross.

"Yes, you do," Neldo reminded him cheerfully. "You know you do, and I can show you where our nest is, too, and where the barn is, because you never want to go anywhere near the barn. Once the snake has eaten he stays full for a long time, but the barn cats never stop hunting even if they're not hungry. So we'll start off heading toward the barn."

If Neldo wasn't going to be a grump, he wouldn't be one, either, Fredle decided. "The inside cat is like that, too," he told her. "It just likes catching mice."

Side by side they darted back across the grass and the rough dirt up to the shelter of one of the garden fence posts. There, they had to catch their breath and couldn't speak for a long while. Then Neldo said, "I want to show you," and they went along the garden fence heading away from the compost pile, until they came to the final post. "Look," Neldo said.

Fredle saw the chickens in their pen, with their own little house, which, since he was color-blind to red, he saw as dark gray. "Why should I look at chickens?" he asked, to show Neldo that he knew chickens when he saw them.

She wasn't a bit upset about that, or surprised. It was as if she thought he already knew everything. "No, look past the chicken pen."

Fredle did as he was told and he saw a large mass in the distance, dark gray, the same color as the chickens' house, but huge. This was probably the same dark mass that he saw when he went out to look at the night sky. "What *is* that?"

"A chicken pen," Neldo told him, "but I said look beyond."

"I am. There's something big, big as the house—"

"Actually, it's bigger."

"With a little white wall on one side—"

"That's our woodshed wall."

"What is it?"

"That's the barn. The cats like to lie in the sun in front of the barn."

Fredle didn't see anything that looked like a cat. "What's a barn for?" he asked, studying the flat-faced building, bigger than the house and as dark as the clouds that carried rain.

"It's where Snake the cat and Fox the cat live, and Mister keeps his tractor in there and his lawn mower and his chain saw, all the machines that cut things down or dig them up. The cows go in there at night, and in winter Mister and Missus keep the sheep behind it. Rats live in the barn, and there are families of mice, too, barn mice. They live on the oats and hay and other feed Mister keeps in there."

"Field mice live in the barn? They live with cats and rats?"

"And the dogs in summer. In summer the dogs like to sleep in the barn."

"Don't field mice have *any* sense of survival?" Fredle asked. "Your family lives near a snake, they live near rats and cats. Why don't field mice live in fields?"

"Live out in fields? In the wild?" Neldo shook her head. "That would be crazy. But I don't know why you're acting so superior. You house mice live with a cat, and traps, and it was eating something bad for you that almost got you went, eating something bad that you found *inside*, where you're claiming it's so much safer."

"But we know when it's safe inside, we know what's safe—mostly. Most of us are safe most of the time." It sounded like they were having a contest. Were he and Neldo competing to see who had the safest territory? Who cared? he wondered, and, What difference did it make?

Neldo apparently felt the same. "You've seen where we live, now, and the barn, so let's go," she said. "Didn't you want to explore around the front of the house?"

By the time they had returned to Fredle's lattice wall, he had another question. "Why don't any other mice have their nests under the porch? Like mine."

Neldo didn't have to even stop to think, it was so obvious. "It's too far from food, especially in winter. But you know what? You're right, Fredle. In winter you'll be protected from snow—"

Fredle stopped himself from interrupting to ask her what *snow* was.

"—just like we are in the woodshed."

"Let's go," Fredle said, suddenly impatient with all the talking. "You lead."

They went on through bright midday sun, moving along close to the lattice wall. The grass shone green, the lattice wall shone white, and the air glimmered all around. Then they went around a sharp corner and the lattice was gone. Neldo went right on, but Fredle hesitated, looking back for places to run to for shelter, looking around, looking forward.

That was when he saw something he could never have imagined, right in front of him, something as surprising as stars.

"Oh," said Fredle. "Oh my."

They were tall, and straight-stemmed, with two long wings of leaves rising up along the stem. The warm air near them was filled with a faint sweet smell and the stems held up tall cups, in different colors, white and yellow and the same dark gray as the barn, but shiny. That dark gray didn't hold his eyes, but the white and yellow did, where they glowed in their loveliness.

Fredle stood struck still, and looked. Row behind row, there were three straight rows of these shining things, standing in the sunlight. He looked up at the smooth-sided cups and then his eyes ran down the long green stems, then they flew up on the winglike dark green leaves. Did those cups catch the rain when it fell? he wondered. Were they there for the humans to bend and drink out of? He thought that water held in those cups, especially the white ones, would have a power no other water could match. He thought that if a mouse could drink that water he would become more of a mouse than he had been, wiser perhaps if he drank from the white cup, stronger and faster, maybe, if from the yellow cup. And if he drank out of the dark gray cup, what power would he learn?

Neldo woke him from his dreaming thoughts with a sharp poke of the nose. "Come on! You can't just— Don't stand around in the open like that! What's *wrong* with you, Fredle?"

She was dancing on her four little feet, as restless as Bardo.

"What are they?" Fredle asked.

"You mean these flowers? I don't know—get moving, Fredle!—roses, maybe, or tulips or daisies, it doesn't matter, they're not good to eat. Come *on*!"

Fredle caught her nervousness and skittered after her into the shelter of the row of flowers growing closest to the wall of the house. He made himself pay attention to what was in front of his eyes, but it was an effort not to turn his head to look at and smell the flowers. *Next time*, he promised himself. *Next time I'll come alone so I can look as long as I want to.*

As if she could know what he was thinking, Neldo said, "Next time we'll come just to look at the flowers. Early in the day, the dew on their petals catches the light and it's as if the flowers have been sprinkled with stars."

"Oh," said Fredle again, as he tried to imagine that.

"You'll see," she assured him. "But right now, aren't we looking for a way to get through the foundation?"

"What's the foundation?"

"It's what the house rests on. It's these big, hard stones, and the humans put mortar between them to seal them closed. The foundation is what keeps the bad weather out of the house, too. The barn has a foundation but the woodshed doesn't, and neither does the chicken coop."

"I just don't know enough," Fredle said. He wished there wasn't so much to know.

"Yes you do," Neldo answered. "But you know about inside, not outside. But you're learning about outside, and you do already know a lot. Even Bardo says so."

They were walking along, studying the stony wall beside them, noses close to the bottom, where the foundation met dirt. These stones were impenetrable. The mortar between them was sometimes crumbly, but the two mice found no opening, no way in. After a while, their progress was halted by a wooden wall.

"Steps?" Fredle guessed.

"See? What did I tell you? You do know things."

"*Are* these steps?"

"I think so. Probably. They look like the other steps, don't you think? But this is the farthest I've ever gone, around the house. I don't know *what* comes next." She hesitated, then asked, "Do you want to keep going?"

Fredle did.

Single file, they went along the edge of the steps, Neldo in the lead, but found no cracks or openings in the wood. They had just passed the first corner, where the steps came down to the ground, and were crossing over stones that were small and sharp enough to make the going uncomfortable, when Fredle heard a hissing, purring sound.

He froze.

"Well, well," said a soft voice.

Neldo had disappeared.

"What have we here?"

Fredle turned his head, just slightly, just enough to glimpse—exactly what he feared. A cat. He knew this cat. It was the kitchen cat, a long-legged, orange-colored, yellow-eyed beast that all the mice knew hunted only for the fun of it, just to catch and went mice and not because it was hungry. Missus fed that cat its own food in its own bowl. All the mice knew that, because when there was no other choice they sometimes raided that bowl.

The orange cat was crouching, low, ready. Its tail—the end twitching—swept the ground. Fredle looked around desperately.

There was no shelter. Where was Neldo hiding? There was no sound except for a distant barking and some insect, humming happily to itself.

"Why are you doing this?" he asked the cat, still without moving. Any mouse knew that the moment you moved, the cat pounced. "It's not as if Missus doesn't give you enough food."

"I might as well ask what you're doing outside, a fat, healthy house mouse like you."

"We never hurt you," Fredle said.

"You've taken my food out of my bowl," the cat answered.

So he was going to have to make a run for it. Fredle knew that, and he knew how slim his chances were. What he didn't know was what way to run—ahead was unknown and behind there was no place for a mouse to hide from a cat except among the tall flowers, which would offer little protection.

Back or forward? Forward or back? He couldn't decide. But he had to get moving because if he didn't, he had no chance at all.

Back, he decided, since he'd rather went among those flowers than anywhere else, and he tensed his—

"Patches! Hello, Patches! You're outside! Do you want to play?" barked Sadie, bouncing across the grass toward the cat, with Angus following. "Look, Angus, it's Patches! He's outside!"

Fredle took advantage of the cat's momentary inattention to back away, slowly, slowly, toward the flowers. He didn't even notice the sharp stones cutting into his paws.

"I'm—" hissed the cat. Sadie's head was now between the cat and Fredle. The cat's tail waved angrily. "I'm hunting, can't you see?"

Fredle crept two more steps backward.

"But, Patches, you only hunt inside. Snake and Fox are the outside hunters."

"Don't you know that about cats, Sadie?" asked Angus. "Cats hunt wherever they are, all the time. It's what cats do."

"Oh," Sadie said. She turned to Fredle, who halted in mid-creep. "Do you live under the back porch?" she asked him.

"That's not me," he said.

"Yes it is. I can smell it. But you don't smell like a field mouse. A field mouse smells wilder, different, smells like grass and—" Her noise pointed into the rows of flowers. "There's a field mouse hiding in there," she told Fredle.

"So what if I *am* under the porch?" Fredle said, to distract her from Neldo.

"What's your name?" asked Sadie, but before he could answer she told him, "I'm Sadie and that's Angus and this is Patches. I know this mouse," she said to the cat. "I wish you wouldn't hunt him."

"Dogs don't *know* mice," Patches answered, but the cat was no longer crouching. He sat up and curled his tail around himself, as if he couldn't care less about anything and especially about any mouse who might happen to be nearby.

"Dogs don't know cats, either," Angus remarked. "I've told her that, lots of times, but she doesn't listen. She never listens to me."

"Yes I do," Sadie protested. "Just not when you're wrong." She turned back to Fredle. "What *is* your name, or don't mice have names?"

"We do," Fredle told her, adding, "Fredle."

93

"Hello, Fredle," Sadie said. "Do you want to play? You can run and we can all hunt you."

"Not in Missus's flowers," Angus warned Sadie. "You know the rules, not in the flowers."

Fredle was going to have to explain things to this Sadie dog, who didn't seem to know who was who in the food chain. "You're too big for me to play with. It wouldn't be fun for either one of us." Fredle was thinking that it especially wouldn't be any fun for *him*, trying to survive hunting games with giants, and one of them a cat.

"Oh." Sadie was disappointed, but she accepted his decision. She lowered her head to the ground, her black nose pointing toward him. "I guess so. We have a baby."

"I know," he said. "Can I go now?"

"If you have to," Sadie said.

Fredle looked at Patches. The yellow eyes stared back at him.

Fredle waited.

"Oh, all right," Patches said.

"You wouldn't eat one of my other friends, would you, Patches?" Sadie was asking the cat as Fredle broke into a full scurry. He tucked himself into the corner where the steps met the foundation stones, and huddled there, shivering.

After a while, he heard the dogs go away. After another while, he heard the sound of the cat padding back up the steps. Only then did Neldo creep out from among the flowers to join him in his corner. For a long time, all they could do was look at one another, amazed that they were both alive.

Finally Neldo asked, "How did you *do* that?"

"Do what?"

"Get away from the cat."

"I didn't. You heard what happened, you saw. Sadie saved me."

"She knows who you are. How did you get to know a dog? I wondered why you didn't run, the way mice are supposed to, but that explains it. I guess things really *are* different inside."

"You ran away," Fredle remembered now. "You didn't even warn me."

"That's what mice are supposed to do, run. First you run and then—if you make it—you hide. What's to talk about?"

"I didn't say talk, I said warn. You didn't even poke me."

"It wouldn't have done any good," Neldo told him. She didn't sound a bit sorry. "You were frozen there, not moving a whisker, like a went mouse. I'd just have been eaten, too."

Fredle had been thinking, while his shivering slowed down to the occasional shudder. "I was lucky."

"Well," said Neldo, "you seem to be a pretty lucky mouse in general. The dog saves you from the cat. Missus carries you outside when your family tries to went you. If that's not luck, what is it?"

Fredle couldn't disagree, but he still minded the way Neldo had just bolted off, without even giving him a warning nudge, so he kept up the quarrel. "Didn't I just say that?"

9

Helping Sadie

Over the next days, Fredle explored the front of the house, and then he went to the side beyond that, which had neither porch nor steps nor flowers, although there were green bushes growing close to the foundation where a mouse could hide. Often Neldo was with him, and then he learned about trees, and the long-haired, mouselike creatures called squirrels, who ran up and down the trunks, faster than anything Fredle had ever seen. Just as often, however, he went on his own. Alone or in Neldo's company, he took time to admire the flowers. Going along the foundation one day, the two mice came to something new and different, something not stones and mortar, and not wood, either, although the glass center had wood all around it.

"It's a window." Neldo anticipated his next question. "I

don't know what they're for or what this smooth part is. Windows are something humans have."

"It's glass," Fredle told her.

"Glass?"

"It's hard and you can see through it. Mister and Missus could see the grass through these windows. They could go down into the cellar and look at the grass," Fredle said, "and the trees, too." If he'd been a human, he'd have put a window where he could see the flowers through it.

"What's a cellar?" asked Neldo.

As he studied the wood around the window, which struck him as a likely place for mouse-sized cracks to appear, Fredle told her about the way the inside of the house was built, one floor on top of the other, all of it resting on the cellar. "I've never actually been to the cellar."

"Then how do you know it's there?" asked Neldo.

"I don't," Fredle admitted. "But I think it is. Because the walls keep going on down," he explained. "The walls don't stop at the floor, inside."

They found no cracks, no openings into inside. Fredle looked through the window but could see only darkness. As they came to the end of the wooden window frame, he asked, "Are there any more of these?"

"I don't know." Then Neldo said, "But, Fredle? I've been thinking. If you go back inside you won't see me anymore."

"That would be the plan," Fredle told her, but right away he had second thoughts, because he did enjoy her company. "You know," he said, "if I can get back in, then I can come out again, too."

"Would you do that?" asked Neldo.

"Probably not." Fredle hadn't realized that. He asked Neldo, "Would you like to come inside with me?"

"Nunh-uh." She was vehement. "I couldn't live anywhere as dangerous as inside. Everybody says house mice have it easy but I don't believe that."

"Neldo," he reminded her, "you live in the same woodshed as a snake."

"But we know the snake. We know his habits, and besides, the snake only eats one mouse at a time. Never more than one. He's not like the cats."

"I guess no mouse has an easy life." This was what Fredle was coming to understand, that no mouse has it easy, despite whatever other mice might think and say.

By then, the two mice had come up to another small, low window, equally dark, equally well-sealed-off as far as Fredle could see, and it was time to turn back, he knew, time to return to their own side of the house. He was looking forward to seeing those flowers again. He always looked forward to seeing the flowers. The stars, too; he always looked forward to seeing the stars floating in the dark night air, and he enjoyed watching the wandering moons as they came and went, their gleaming whiteness, their various shapes and sizes, each one different from the others. It wasn't only Neldo he wouldn't see again when he found a way to get back inside, he realized.

That night, as he sat looking up at the sky, contentedly alone and admiring, Fredle noticed a darkness—like a cloud but not at all like a cloud—in the air above him, a darkness closer than the stars and moons.

Without hesitation, as if he had been born and bred outside, Fredle ran, and—as if he had somehow made a mental note of this without even paying attention, like a genuine field mouse—he ran to the steps, not to his lattice wall. The steps were the nearest shelter.

A dark shape fell out of the air, wings spread wide, toward the spot where he had been standing until just two seconds ago. There was a rushing sound, like wind, and a short, irritated squawk, and then the darkness rose upward again.

Fredle watched it go off. He was just as frightened as he should have been, which was very frightened indeed. Maybe it was an owl, maybe a hawk, maybe an eagle. It could have been anything that hunted by night, but he knew that if he hadn't been looking up at the stars, he'd never have seen it in time.

After that, he was careful to always occupy a different position for his skygazing. Raptors, he guessed, like mice, were creatures of habit. That bird must have seen him there more than once before it decided to attack. Fredle could have stopped going out into the night, but he wasn't about to *not* look at the stars, and the moons. He understood now that once he found his way back inside, he'd never see them again.

Not many days after that, Bardo and Neldo and Fredle were all foraging together on the compost. Fredle was thinking that later, after a short rest, he would head off along the foundation in a new direction. Not knowing what he might find there, hoping that he might come upon a way in, gave him a bright feeling, eagerness and excitement and just enough fear to make it an adventure.

"I'm going to explore past the garbage cans," he announced. "Around the fourth side. Do you want to come?"

"Not me," Bardo said.

"Me either," Neldo said. "I don't go there. The cats go hunting around that side of the house once the weather gets warm."

"If even Neldo stays clear, you better believe it's dangerous, chum," Bardo agreed. "I can tell you that I've seen with my own eyes Fox coming around the corner with a fat, frightened gray house mouse in his jaws."

"Some of them get away," Neldo said.

"Even if they do, no house mouse lasts long out here. So I would advise against heading off in that direction, young Fredle."

Fredle pretended to be concentrating on an eggshell, which had the advantage of being very light and thus easy to move around, with the disadvantage of being difficult to chew. But really, he was thinking about what Bardo had just told him, without meaning to. Fredle could draw the logical conclusion: if the barn cats came around from that fourth side of the house carrying a house mouse, then there was a way in. He could be sure that the cats must know how to get into the house because he absolutely knew that no house mouse would voluntarily venture outside.

"I'll spare you the disappointment," Bardo said. "Eggshells aren't worth the trouble of chewing them up."

Fredle turned his attention to a dark gray strip of apple peel. "What is that chicken feed you all go foraging for?" he asked.

"Corn," Neldo said.

"Neldo," Bardo warned her. "You know the rules."

"What difference does it make if he knows? Haven't you figured it out yet? He's not going to try to share our food. He just wants to survive out here until he can get back inside. He's no danger to us, Bardo." She turned back to Fredle. "Plus there are brown things, like the dogs get only much smaller, some kind of kibbles, and something gritty and pale, like dirt. We never eat that. But the chickens like it; chickens will eat anything, they just peck away at the ground and swallow whatever comes up. They'll eat *bugs*. Ick-ko."

"Do they eat mice?" asked Fredle, since *anything* included mice and it was easy to see that a mouse was a lot smaller than a chicken.

"Ha-ha, very funny," said Bardo. "But you don't want to get between a chicken and its food. A good strike with one of those beaks and a chicken will cripple you, and chances are you'll be dinner for the snake before you know it."

Fredle didn't respond. He finished his strip of apple peel and set off. As he came up to the garden gate post he saw the large figure of Missus, approaching. Fredle froze.

Missus carried a basket in one hand and the bucket in the other. Sadie bounded along beside her. "We're working! Weeding the garden! Feeding the chickens! Taking care of the baby! It's warm and sun—" Sadie fell silent, sniffing the air, and then she said quietly, "Hello, Fredle. My job is to watch the baby." She went to the basket Missus had set down just inside the garden fence and sat in the dirt beside it. "Do you want to see our baby? I could lift you in my mouth but you have to be quiet."

However, Missus leaned down to stretch a thin cloth over the top of the basket before she went off into the garden, so Fredle couldn't have seen the baby even if he had trusted Sadie to put him up in her mouth and not eat him. He tried to explain it to her. "It's not safe for a mouse to be near humans." *Or dogs*, he didn't add.

"The baby can't hurt you. Not yet, anyway, because babies can't do anything, not even pull my ears. That's why I have to be her nanny."

Fredle stayed crouched behind his post. "Where's Angus?"

"When Mister checks the sheep in their pasture, Angus helps him. Sometimes I help, too, but not today." Sadie lay down beside the baby's basket, which wasn't really a basket at all but more like a box with a handle, and pointed her nose at the post behind which Fredle hid. "What are you doing here?"

"I was foraging in the compost."

"You don't eat compost, do you? Ick-ko."

"It's better than your kibbles."

"You eat my kibbles?"

"Not when they're in the bowl," Fredle assured her quickly, in case—like Patches—the dogs resented it if a mouse took the food from their bowls. "But sometimes you spill them."

"I'm thirsty," Sadie said, a little sadly. "I want a drink of water. I want to go get a drink from the stream and chase a frog. Have you ever smelled a frog? The stream isn't far, just across the field, and I can run fast. I can run very fast," she told Fredle, and sighed. "But I have a job." Then, "I have a job!" she told Fredle, proudly.

Fredle was feeling a little thirsty, too, now that the subject had come up, and he thought that a juicy apple peel would refresh him.

"Are you going? Will you come back?"

"If I can," Fredle said.

Bardo and Neldo were no longer at the compost, and he went quickly to the part of the pile where he'd noticed more apple peels—which he hadn't mentioned to his two companions, although neither had he tried to hide it from them. On his way back to the lattice he stopped to talk with Sadie, but she had fallen asleep and was snoring gently. He was about to move on when Missus approached and Sadie leapt up with a short, happy bark.

"Sadie? Sit," Missus said, in a stern voice. "I'm going to feed the chickens. You stay with the baby."

Sadie lay down again beside the basket. Fredle had never eaten corn, so he started to follow Missus toward the chicken pen, coming cautiously out from behind the shelter of his fence post. Luckily for him, he hadn't taken many steps before he looked up and sighted two cats ahead. He froze.

One of the cats was large and all white. The other was large, too, but black-and-white. *The barn cats,* he thought. They stalked through the sunlight in front of the open barn door. They were coming toward the garden.

The cats hadn't seen him. Slowly, watching the cats, he backed up the short distance to the safety of the fence post near which Sadie slept beside the baby in its basket.

The cats stretched lazily in the sunlight and then strode side by side along by the woodshed. From this angle, Fredle could see into Neldo's home. He noticed that only a few logs were piled up in it and that there might have been—but it might also have been only his fears taking a shape—something long and dark, darker even than the dark gray barn, hanging down from the ceiling. The cats paid no mind to any of that. They turned toward the chicken pen.

When they caught sight of the cats, the chickens squawked and darted up into the air with their wings outspread and flapping. Not being able to fly, the chickens ran away from the cats, who went right up to the fence and stared in at them, fat cat tails raised, backs arched, sharp teeth showing as they hissed.

"Shoo!" said Missus. "Get away, cats! Shoo!"

The cats yawned.

Missus dashed right at them, waving her bucket. "I mean it! Shoo!"

Slowly, to show Missus that they were doing it because they wanted to, not because she told them to, the cats moved off. They went in different directions. The white one came toward the garden while the black-and-white one went back to sit in the dirt and scratch itself, right in front of the woodshed.

From behind his post, Fredle now watched the white cat, which was moving slowly, lazily, silently, through the grass, its attention fixed on something in the garden. What something was it stalking? Fredle wondered.

When Fredle turned his head—just slightly because cats could perceive the smallest of movements, even the smallest movements of mice—he saw that it was Sadie toward whom the cat was heading, and that was a relief.

Sadie lay beside the basket with her nose on her paws and her eyes closed. Her ears were raised, but they were always raised, so that might not mean anything. Next to her, little noises came out of the basket and the light cloth that Missus had spread over the top of it rose and fell. It looked as if a giant mouse was running along upside down underneath that cloth. This was what the cat had seen and was curious to find out about.

The cat came up to the basket, and then circled around until it stood on the far side, across from Sadie. It watched the cloth moving. The cloth rippled and the cat watched. Then the cat sank down, tensed its muscles, and crouched, concentrating on whatever it was that moved like that and made those sounds. Its tail waved slowly, back and forth, against the ground.

For just a few seconds, Fredle was undecided. He had been taught to freeze, but then he had also been advised to run, here outside. Moreover, Sadie had saved him from Patches. Taking care of the baby was Sadie's responsibility and Fredle wanted to help her, even if she was a dog.

It wasn't even a few seconds, it was only two or three, that Fredle hesitated. The cat was crouched, ready to spring, and Fredle moved. He dashed out from cover and ran toward the sleeping dog, as quick as any squirrel and not even looking to see if the cat had noticed him.

No clawed cat paw landed on top of him. No victorious screech sounded. He made it safely to his destination, which was the soft part right under Sadie's shoulder. He stuck his nose in there and gave her a quick nip.

With a yowl, Sadie jumped up, fully awake. Fredle had to

get himself quickly into the shelter of the baby's basket or she might have knocked him around.

He knew she hadn't seen him. He also knew—by the sound of her furious barking—that she *did* see the cat, right away.

"Get out of here, Fox! You get away from Baby or—"

"Or what?" came a mocking voice.

Anxious, Fredle crept along until he could see what was happening. He saw that the cat had abandoned its hunter's crouch and was once again standing, back arched, tail fat, hissing at the brown-and-white dog.

"Out!" barked Sadie. Then she bared her teeth and snarled. "Get out!"

"As if I'd ever be afraid of you," said Fox, but he stalked off, head held high.

The baby was howling now.

"And stay away. You better!" barked Sadie.

Missus came running up to the fence, still holding the bucket of chicken feed. She looked at Sadie. "What's wrong, girl? What is it?" She bent down and took the cloth off the baby's basket. "Hello, Baby, don't cry, it's just Sadie barking and that's what dogs do. Everything's all right."

"I saved the baby!"

"Quiet, Sadie, there's nothing. Baby doesn't like all that barking."

"Fox was going to—"

"Quiet, Sadie," said Missus firmly.

Sadie stopped barking. She lay down again, beside the basket, and rested her head on her paws, looking up at Missus.

"Good dog. I won't be much longer," said Missus, and she walked away.

Sadie had started sniffing. She lifted her head. "Fredle?"

"I bit you," said Fredle. "I'm sorry if it hurt, but that cat—"

"I saved the baby!"

"I saw."

"That was Fox and he's a bad one."

"I could tell."

"Don't bite me again," Sadie said.

"I needed to wake you up."

"Friends don't bite," Sadie told him. "Angus never bites me, not even when we're wrestling and quarreling. And I don't bite him, or any other friend."

"All right," said Fredle. "I understand, it's a rule."

"I'd bite that Fox," Sadie said, growling at the memory. "I'm glad you woke me up, but I'd never bite Patches. Patches is my friend."

Fredle went back to the protection of the post and waited there until Missus had come to pick up the baby and gone off, back to the house, with Sadie at her heels. Then he returned to his nest, to curl up for a short sleep. He wanted to be well rested when he went out looking for a way into the house, on the fourth and final side, where nobody had ever searched before, at least as far as he knew.

10
The Way In

It was night when Fredle found a way back into the house. Just as he had suspected, and hoped, one of the wooden window frames on the fourth side of the house had pulled away from the mortar, leaving a crack large enough for a mouse. He pushed his nose into the opening and sniffed the air.

Only a mouse could squeeze through that narrow opening, Fredle knew; or ants and spiders, which didn't worry him; or a snake, he guessed, if snakes ever wanted to go inside. But he'd never heard anything about any snake living down in the cellar. He was just scaring himself. He smelled the familiar odor of damp ground and other things, too, soap smells and wood smells and human smells, also an unpleasant heavy odor. He lifted his nose. Was there just a hint of food? What food could there be in a cellar?

He stuck his head in, to look and listen. All he could see was darkness, although in the distance there was a faint gray window shape, almost light. What he heard was the kind of silence that comes when many small noises mix together, none of them human, none of them clumsy and loud and doggy. Here inside no wind whistled. The air lay still.

Fredle shoved until his shoulders and front legs were inside. The ground below felt close, and as his eyes grew accustomed to the dense darkness, he thought he could see, just below him, a more solid blackness, which was earth, not air. He reached a paw down—careful not to lose his balance. If he was wrong about how close the ground was, and if he fell, tumbling through empty air until he hit hard bottom, he could hurt himself so badly that he would just lie there, unable to move, until he was went. However, reaching down, he felt the familiar soft, cool touch of dirt, so he wriggled through until he stood on all four paws in darkness.

Far ahead lay that dimness, the kind of dim light he remembered from his home behind the pantry wall, not really light at all, just not darkness. Turning to look behind him, he saw through the glass of the window to the clear night air outside, where there were no walls to lock the darkness in, where spaces stretched endlessly and, in not very long, one of the moons might make an appearance among the stars.

He could go home now. No other mouse had ever went and then come back again, but Fredle was about to. He had never in his life felt so clever, and the happiness and pride he was feeling were almost more than could be contained in one small body. He wanted to jump in circles; he wished he could bark like Sadie, or fly like a crow, soar up into the air with happiness.

Then he thought of something not so happy; he thought of leaving outside. He wished he could say goodbye to Neldo before he returned home, and even Bardo, too. That was probably not possible, but he wouldn't mind taking a last look at the stars, and the cupped flowers—

No, the flowers were too far away. It would be foolhardy to go around front, and besides, it was a dark night and he wouldn't be able to see their colors. The stars, however, were just beyond the window and so Fredle scrambled back out through the crack.

That night, the stars were hidden behind clouds that rushed across the sky, running after the wind. Fredle was surprised at how disappointed he was, not to see them. The way in, he thought, staring up in a vain attempt to catch a glimpse of even one single white brightness, would not move, would not close. It would wait. Maybe he should go foraging in the compost and then go back to his own small nest and wait until a cloudless night before he returned inside. If he did that, he would be able to see the flowers one more time, too, and maybe even have a chance to tell Sadie what he was doing.

Fredle knew that to wait was not necessarily a smart choice, although he couldn't see that it was particularly stupid. He decided, therefore, not to decide right then. Instead, he decided to go to the compost and say goodbye to Neldo, if she was there, and Bardo. And if they weren't there? Better to decide everything on a full stomach, he decided, and he set off.

The wind whispered in his ears as he scurried, keeping

close to the foundation. He went through low bushes, past the other low window on the fourth side of the house, through more bushes, and around the corner to the protection of the garbage cans, where he would start his dash—at night, you were foolish not to cross open spaces at your best speed—across the road and grass to the safety of the garden fence post. Inside, he remembered, there were no raptors, and no wind and rain, either. In the adventure of being outside, he had almost forgotten how comfortable life could be inside, and how safe.

Just as Fredle reached the corner, there came an outburst of furious barking. He froze, close up to the stone foundation, safely hidden—or so he hoped—behind the thick branches of one of the low bushes. He recognized Sadie's bark, high and happy, and then Angus's, which was lower and louder, more serious, more threatening.

"Robbers!" Angus half barked, half snarled. "Out! Out!"

"We *see* you!" barked Sadie, cheerfully.

A scurrying sound mixed in with the wind's whisper, and then Fredle heard a thump. A high, nasal voice said, "Cheese it, guys. It's the dogs!"

"I'm warning you," snarled Angus. "You thieving sneaks, get out!" he barked.

There was more scurrying.

"Look how fast they run," said Sadie. "Let's catch them!"

"Try it. Just you try it," growled the nasal voice, which now sounded dangerous and full of teeth.

"No, Sadie, don't follow them." Angus was quieter now. "You know what'll happen."

"But those aren't skunks."

"They're more dangerous than skunks," Angus said. "Mister says. Mister'll be here"—and he barked three times, sharply—"any minute."

Sadie echoed his barks. "We're here! Mister! We're in the garbage!"

Fredle heard the kitchen door bang and quick footsteps of a human on the porch, on the steps, and then Mister said, "Good dogs. Angus? Come! Sadie? Come!"

"We chased them away!" barked Sadie.

"Quiet, girl. Good job, both of you. Let me turn this flashlight on and we'll do a check."

"Yes, check," said Angus. "Check the barn, check the garden, check the chickens."

"A flashlight!" Sadie barked, more excited than before. "I can dance! I can be the dancing dog!"

Angus growled impatiently. "This isn't a game, Sadie. This is serious."

Fredle was so curious about all this that he forgot to be afraid. He crept close enough to see the two dogs, who were standing near the garbage containers. The man was coming toward them, following a stream of light.

"I'll check the garden with Mister," Angus said. "You guard the garbage."

Fredle saw one dark dog shape run off, and he saw a garbage can lying on its side. Sadie had her nose in the contents, which were spread around on the ground.

Suddenly Angus turned and came back. "Don't eat any of that. You're not hungry." He ran off again.

"Maybe I am," Sadie said softly, continuing to sniff and snuffle. "I won't eat if I'm not supposed to, but I can still be hungry. What are you doing here, Fredle? It wasn't you, was it? Did you knock over the garbage? Are you friends with the raccoons?"

"There were raccoons?" answered Fredle. "I didn't see them."

"We chased them off. They're frightened of us. They know how to take the top off a garbage can and now there's a big mess."

Lured by all the good food odors, Fredle came closer. He was smelling flavors he'd noticed in the air of the kitchen at night, after the humans had gone away, some of them delicious in ways he'd never smelled before. There was even something sweet and—

"Chicken bones are bad for you," Sadie warned him.

Fredle had tracked the sweetness down to a pale, round paper container. "What's this?"

"Ice cream." She stuck her nose down to smell it. "We aren't allowed ice cream and neither is the baby."

"Is it poisonous?" It didn't smell poisonous and it didn't smell like that dark brown chocolate, either. Fredle crept up to the rim of the round container lying on its side on the ground.

"Because of all the sugar. Patches doesn't like sugar, but I wish—and there are nuts in it, too," Sadie said, with longing. "I'm not allowed," she told Fredle.

Fredle crept over the rim and down into the container, to where the ice cream puddled.

"Sadie!" barked Angus. "I said, don't eat anything!"

"I wasn't, I was just—"

"Angus and Sadie, come!" Mister called. The light showed Angus running back toward Sadie. "I'll get this mess picked up later," Mister said, "but first we have to check the garden. We can't let raccoons destroy the vegetable crop."

"Wait for me!" Sadie barked, and she followed Mister off into the darkness.

Fredle didn't notice them leaving. He had taken his first taste of ice cream and forgotten about everything else. It was so creamy sweet and nutty sweet, all he could be was tasting it.

So deep had Fredle sunk into the deliciousness of ice cream that he barely heard the dogs barking in the garden. He filled his mouth and tasted. He was so concentrated on sweetness that he didn't hear the whispering voices or the soft steps that approached as soon as the dogs had gone. If he had been paying attention to anything other than ice cream, he would have heard this conversation:

"It's not like that's the only ice cream container you'll ever see, Cap'n."

"It's the only one right here right now."

"The farmer could come back any minute."

"I'll risk it."

"The dogs."

"Those dogs—they're *pets*. If you're so nervous, you can wait here."

"You know me better than that, Cap'n. I'm not nervous."

"You could fool me, Rad. In fact, you *are* fooling me."

"Cap'n, be—"

And Fredle was knocked down onto the bottom of the

container, into a puddle of ice cream, and then in a rush he felt himself rising—carried in the container—up into the air. At first it felt the same as when Missus had trapped him and taken him outside, but after that everything was different.

The container was moving so fast and so unevenly that he couldn't get his feet under him to look up and see what was going on. Now he did hear the voices.

"You're brave, Cap'n, but still— Hey, they didn't wait for us. Let's get out of here. It's a good thing that farmer went to check the garden first."

Above his head, Fredle heard a strangled sound: "Gugg-huh?"

"No, no gun. Another good thing. I hope there's enough ice cream to make it worth the chance you took. I don't want to have to fight off everyone else to get my fair share."

After that, Fredle's ride became, while no more comfortable, at least rhythmic. He slipped from side to side in the container at regular intervals, while also bouncing up and down with equal regularity. His feet could find no purchase in the ice cream, so he couldn't get his balance for long enough to look up to see what it was that was carrying him. Not a human, he knew, and not a dog. Besides, he didn't really need to see what it might be. He had his suspicions, and they were not happy ones. He remembered his mother's worried voice: *Will you never learn that your sweet tooth gets you in trouble?*

Gradually he became frightened, and his fear grew into terror as the journey went on, and on. His legs wanted to run in panic, but they couldn't. Bouncing made it impossible for his nails to grip, and besides, it was painfully, terrifyingly obvious to him that even if he could get a grip and run, there was nowhere to run to.

It continued on, this blind, helpless journey. Where would it end?

It would end in went, he couldn't help but know that. He heard little squeaking sounds coming out of his mouth.

And still he was carried along. In one way, Fredle wanted the journey never to end, but with each bounce, each slide, his fear expanded, until he thought his whole body would explode. His heart beat so fast he almost couldn't see, and he knew he couldn't hear anything except for the wild pounding of his heart.

Fredle had been afraid many times in his life, out foraging in the kitchen, climbing up walls behind Axle, and especially when he'd been so sick and they had all joined together to push him out. After that he'd been afraid alone, outside, day after day. But this was a worse fear, larger and darker and unending, all-encompassing—

Until suddenly, unexpectedly, fear left him.

Fredle felt himself growing calm. His heart slowed, his ears opened. It wasn't that he had stopped being bounced about, being slid from side to side, and it wasn't that he had thought of a way to escape; neither of those had happened. Nothing had changed in his situation. But something had changed in Fredle.

He knew what was going to happen and he knew how bad it was, and that was that. He didn't know for sure what creature had captured him but he suspected raccoons. So if it was any consolation, he would see a raccoon before he went.

It was no consolation.

He didn't know how long he had to live, either, and about that he had no way to even guess. All he could do was wait, and so he did.

Finally the container stopped moving. It dropped down onto the ground, and then Fredle could look up. When he did, he saw a large, hairy face with a short, pointed snout and bright little black eyes gleaming out of a wide black stripe.

The head was so big that he couldn't see its ears. He *could* see the whiteness of teeth, as the mouth opened. "Whazzis?" it asked in the nasal voice Fredle had heard earlier. The eyes stared down at Fredle. "C'mere, Rad. C'mere and look what I've caught."

That face withdrew and another, identical to the first, took its place. "Tell me it's not a mouse," a different voice said. "You caught us a mouse, Cap'n. Rimble, you ever seen a mouse close to? You wanna take a look? You ever tasted fresh mouse?"

What was probably a third face appeared, although it could have been either of the first two. Fredle couldn't tell them apart. "Good work, Cap'n," it said.

"That's why I'm the boss," said the first voice, Cap'n.

"Pity I'm not hungry," said the second, Rad.

"I'm hungry," said a fourth, and was immediately answered by the others: "Doesn't count, Rec." "You're always hungry, Woo-Hah."

Even if he couldn't see them, Fredle could hear them, but he couldn't have spoken, even if they had asked him to. He had forgotten every word he ever knew.

"So you all say, but what I say is, you never know where

your next meal is coming from," Rec answered.

"How long's it been since we got ice cream?" asked the third voice, Rimble's, Fredle guessed. "And now we've got ice cream plus a mouse. I've said it before and I say it again, there's nobody like the Cap'n. Here's to Cap'n Rilf, hurrah!" he said. "Smartest raccoon on both sides of the mountain!"

At least, Fredle thought, he'd been right about them being raccoons.

"The mouse is just luck," Rilf admitted.

"I hate not to be hungry when there's mouse on the menu," Rad said. "And a house mouse, by the size of him."

"We all know that after this they'll be extra careful about the tops on the garbage cans for a while," Rec observed, "so we better fill ourselves up while we can. The garden's just being planted, the dogs are outside more, and finding food's not going to get any easier."

"Yeah, but we'll be heading off to the lake, now it's getting warm again, right, Cap'n?" asked Rad. "It's not long now and there's plenty to eat there. Remember fish?"

"I haven't noticed that it's ever easy finding food," Rimble pointed out. "Here or there, it's hard work."

"This mouse is mine," Rilf announced.

"If you say so," they answered reluctantly.

"It's mine and we don't eat it until I say so. Got it?"

"Yessir, Cap'n," they answered, and one of them knocked the container over on its side, then picked it up from the bottom, and Fredle tumbled out into the raccoon-filled night.

Crouching as close as he could get to the ground—as if that would make him less visible—Fredle looked up at four hairy faces, each one with a black band around two bright black eyes. Four narrow snouts pointed down at him, four mouths and four sets of sharp, gleaming teeth.

Fear returned, as strong as before. Fredle huddled on the ground, shivering with terror and wet with ice cream.

The mouths all came at him at the same time. They opened wide, four bright white tooth-filled circles. Then four tongues came out to lick at Fredle, licking all over him, his head and back, stomach, paws. They knocked him around with their big, rough tongues, and rolled him over. They didn't say a word until they had licked him clean. Then one of them picked up the container in his paws and stuck his nose into that for a little while, before passing it on to the raccoon next to him and turning his attention back to Fredle.

They were big, these raccoons. Not as big as the dogs, but to Fredle they looked huge, and he knew that compared to him, they *were* huge.

"I'm Rilf," said the raccoon who had just passed the ice cream carton along. "It's Captain Rilf to you, mouse."

The others were busy passing the container around, each taking a turn.

Fredle couldn't swallow.

"And you'd be?" Rilf asked.

"You don't want to know its name," protested Rad as he passed on the ice cream container.

"Why not?" asked Rec, who Fredle could now see was larger even than his large friends. "You got a problem with eating something whose name you know?"

"Not everyone's a greedyguts, like you," said Rimble.

"Fredle!"

Fredle yelled it out as loud as he could.

If their knowing that he had a name, knowing what that name was, would give him a chance to survive, then he wanted to have that chance. "I'm Fredle!" he yelled again.

11

The Rowdy Boys

"Fredle, is it?" Rilf said. "Well. Pleased to meet you, Fredle."

Seized by a sudden inspiration, Fredle shouted up at the raccoon faces, "I'm inedible!"

This announcement was greeted by silence. Here, wherever it was that they were, with trees looming out of dark shadows—and he smelled stones, too—here the wind was less noticeable, so the silence was all the more loud. Fredle waited to find out if he'd been very smart, or maybe very stupid.

At last, "Woo-Hah," said Rec, who really was about twice as big as the others. "Woo-Hah, Woo-Hah," the others joined in, and Fredle hoped this was raccoon laughter, not raccoon irritation.

Captain Rilf's snout had more silver mixed in with the dark gray-brown than the others, so it shone, slightly, in the pale predawn light. "Fredle inedible? That's incredible," he said. "Woo-Hah."

"Woo-Hah," the others echoed him.

Then the smallest of the four spoke up with youthful enthusiasm. "So, Cap'n, which part do you take? The haunch?" and Rilf answered sharply, "Back off, Rimble. Did you hear me say anything about eating the mouse right now? Did anyone? No, I didn't think so."

"He'll tell us when," said the fourth raccoon, whose round ears were as black as the stripe around his eyes. "You know you don't have to worry about going hungry with the Cap'n in charge."

"Yeah, Rimble. You shouldn't just think about stuffing your face," said Rec, and even Fredle could understand why the others snorted and huffed at this.

"Look who's talking," said Rad.

"Face-stuffer yourself," said Rimble.

Rec growled and took a swipe at the smaller raccoon. Fredle edged closer to Captain Rilf, which he hoped was the safest place to be as Rimble snapped his teeth at Rec, warning him, "Better not."

"Better not what?"

"Fight! Fight!" cheered Rad, but Rilf called a halt to it. "Not now. It's almost morning and nobody's hungry, are they? Are any of you hungry? After a good forage and then ice cream? So why fight over a mouse?"

The two combatants turned to him, their quarrel already forgotten. "It was a good night's pickings," they agreed. "And ice cream. And mouse! You got us quite a night, Cap'n."

"Rec took a cheese wrapper and I saw it first. I called it. It was mine," Rimble complained.

"Squealer," Rec growled.

"He did. You *know* you did, Rec. So he has to give me some of his. Maybe his share of mouse."

"Just you try—"

"Cap'n said none of that, you two," Rad warned them.

Rilf spoke as if he hadn't even heard the new quarrel. "Tonight's food's taken care of without including mouse. I say we introduce ourselves to our new little . . . friend. It's getting light and we'll be bunking down soon." He looked down at Fredle, crouching uneasily near his front paws. "You already know who I am, and this young squirt is Rimble and this great, fat lout—"

Rec made a growling noise.

"—I should say, this big, strong giant of a raccoon—"

"Woo-Hah," they all laughed, even Rec.

"—is Rec, and this is Rad. He's my second in command."

Rimble added, "We're the Rowdy Boys. Everyone knows about us, all over the farm, both sides of the mountain. We're the Rowdy Boys and we're dangerous, so don't try to mess with us."

"Don't be stupid, Rimble," said Rad. "How's a mouse going to mess with *us?*"

"You calling me stupid?" Rimble snarled. "That mouse needs warning."

"Woo-Hah," laughed Rec. "You're scared of something that size? He's barely two mouthfuls apiece, he can't hurt us."

"The mouse has a name, which is Fredle," said Rilf. His

bright, dark eyes studied Fredle. "I'd like to show the girls this fellow. I bet the coonlets could have a good time with him. I'd have loved a mouse when I was little."

"Me too," they all agreed, and then, without a further word to Fredle, they withdrew together into a wide-mouthed burrow dug into the soft ground near some large tree roots and there they curled up, four large, furry bodies, hidden away from sight. In the dim light, they could have been one huge creature, not four separate, smaller ones, except for the way they shoved at one another—"Get your paw out of my eye or I'll bite it off!"—and quarreled—"Try, just you try. I'd like to see you try." "Hey! Cut it out!" "Then don't push me."

Fredle stayed exactly where they'd left him, for a long time, a solitary small gray mouse hunched on a patch of dirt with big trees all around him and a low stone wall nearby. After a while, the air grew lighter. Eventually, all he heard from the burrow was the snoring of sleeping raccoons, which mingled with the sound of the morning breeze rustling branches and leaves. He waited.

Daylight came gently, out in the wild, came slowly. With daylight, Fredle could see what was around him. Trees rose tall, some leafy, others spreading out low branches covered with short, dark green needles. There were clumps of old brown grass, bent flat, and bright green blades of new grass growing among them. The air filled with the voices of birds.

The sounds of birds were very different from the sounds of chickens. Chickens seemed to be chattering away to themselves, but birds conversed. Conversed about *what* Fredle had no idea, but he thought, listening, that one bird would make a noise and another would respond. Their voices were much more pleasant to hear than the cawing of crows.

Fredle could no more have gone to sleep than fly up into the air and talk to birds. His brain was too busy. He thought he must be out in the wild, and he could conclude that the raccoons, like house mice, were nocturnal animals. So his escape—and he certainly did plan to escape before they woke up hungry and caught sight of him—would be best carried out in daylight.

Fredle had no idea where the wild was, how distant from the house, the compost and the garden. He had no idea which direction he should escape into. He wasn't lost, but he very easily might be, and soon, so he wanted to notice everything he could about this particular place. He looked all around.

The low stone wall ran in a straight line through the trees, as far as Fredle could see in both directions. Some of its stones had fallen into the grass that grew beside it. High-limbed, leafy trees and some of the thick, bushy, low-branched trees encircled the small clearing where he stood. He locked the position of everything and of the place itself into his memory, and then he turned to leave it.

"Woo-Hah."

Fredle froze. After a long minute he turned his head to peer at the pile of sleeping raccoons.

Not a one of them stirred. Even Captain Rilf, who slept with his nose pointed toward Fredle, had his eyes tightly closed.

Fredle waited a long, anxious time, while the air brightened around him. Then he ran off, in the direction of the growing light.

The way he had chosen was pathless, and rough with rocks and roots and low bushes. Trees rose up to block his passage. He had to circle around them before he could continue on his way. After a long time, he rounded a thick tree trunk and within six steps knew he could no longer be sure that he was heading on in the same direction. He felt it in his shoulders, the not-knowing, and stopped moving. He retreated to the safety of the tree trunk, to think things over.

But Fredle found that he could only think about being lost. Somehow, in the short distance from one side of the tree trunk to the other, he had gone too far and gotten himself well and truly lost.

This was so uncomfortable a feeling that he went back around the tree, until he knew where he was again. He crouched there to consider the situation.

He had been foolish to just run off like that, just because that way led toward the light. Now he thought that he should have followed the stone wall. Those stone walls were built by humans, so if a mouse followed along one he would eventually come to some other place where humans lived. Where humans lived, there would be mice living, too. Fredle thought now that the wall near which the raccoons had their burrow probably belonged to Mister. After all, the raccoons wouldn't live too far from the source of their food, and the source of their food seemed to be the compost and the garbage cans, both of which belonged to Mister, and therefore, Fredle concluded, the wall, too, must be Mister's. Thus, he decided, if he followed the stone wall he might have a chance of finding the farm again, and the garden, and the way back into the house. The way home.

By the time he got back to the little clearing, it was midday and he was both tired and thirsty. But the raccoons were still asleep, so it was safe for him to approach the wall and try to decide in which direction to run along it.

No instinct told him to go this way, or that. So he simply chose: *this* way.

Even with the stone wall to walk beside, it was hard going. Fredle was full of new hope, however, and he persisted. He went on quite a distance before he began to feel wrong, again, and his hopes began to fade. He knew in his shoulders, just as he had known earlier, that this was the wrong way. Or, rather, he did not know that this was the right way. So he decided to turn back, again, and redirect his steps, again. He didn't know what else he could do. He had no idea where he was, so he had only instinct to guide him home, and all his instinct was saying to him was *wrong*, and *wrong*, and *wrong again*.

At the word *home*, he saw in his imagination the little nest under the porch, and he felt how low and safe the ceiling lay over it, how the lattice wall protected him without closing him in, how spacious and comfortable his territory under the porch had been.

Then he corrected himself. That wasn't home. Home was the wide nest behind the pantry wall, where his father and mother, his grandfather, his brothers and sisters, too, all slept together in the unchanging dim light.

He must be light-headed from hunger, Fredle thought, and tried chewing on some of the blades of new grass that were growing near the wall. They tasted bitter but he ate them anyway before he set off again, back to the raccoons' burrow.

Once more he crossed in front of the pile of sleeping raccoons, their sharp-pointed noses tucked into their sharp-clawed black feet, their bright eyes shut and their browny-gray, silvery-black furry bodies piled up together, so that you couldn't tell where Rimble's shoulder ended and Rec's haunch began. They did not stir as he slipped silently past them and headed off

along the stone wall in the opposite direction, going *that* way, hoping for the best.

By this time, he was hoping for the best but at the same time fearing the worst. He had no idea what to expect, out here, in the wild. He went along as fast as he could, making his way beside the stone wall around and over and through obstacles that had by that time grown familiar. The air was warm, much of the day had gone by, already, and only insects could be heard. Then the wall stopped.

Fredle considered the empty way ahead. It was crossed by a dirt path with long ruts in it, like the road near the house. Could it be some kind of road? And if it was some kind of road, wouldn't it lead him to a house? That is, if he chose the right direction.

The fact was that he had no idea where he was and had no idea how to forage out in the wild. The only thing he knew was how to get back to where the Rowdy Boys slept, and he didn't know what lay in store for him if he did that.

Fredle thought: *Wait a minute. I do know what's in store for me, with those raccoons.*

Then he thought: *I don't think there is anything else I can do.*

So he stopped thinking and turned around, turned back, to make his way to the raccoons' burrow. When he got there, he saw that they were still asleep. Late-afternoon sunlight was turning the air more and more golden, and Fredle, who had been awake for too long a time, was exhausted. He found a little sheltered space between two rough gray stones a good distance from the burrow and curled up there, but he was too miserable to escape into sleep. He closed his eyes, then opened them again.

With his eyes open, he saw that Rilf also had open eyes and was watching him. "You were right the first time," he said, his voice low and growly. "That was the direction to go in, away from the wall, downhill. But you're smart to come back.

It's too far for a mouse to go on his own, through the wild. You'd never have made it."

The eyes closed again. "Go to sleep, mouse."

In his state of hunger and thirst, despair and exhaustion, what else could Fredle do?

12

Living with Raccoons

A thump on the rump jolted Fredle awake. Rilf loomed over him, big and bright-eyed. "Up and at 'em, young Fredle. Thirsty?" he asked. "Hungry?"

Fredle nodded. His mouth was, in fact, too dry for speaking out of, but at least he was no longer exhausted. After all the time he'd lived outside, he was accustomed to sleeping in bits and patches, day or night, so he had had a refreshing rest.

Rilf lowered his snout to the ground beside Fredle. "Climb up, get behind an ear, and hold tight. And I mean *tight*. I'm not sure I'd hear you cry for help if you bounced off, and I know you're too light for me to feel. As long as you don't dig those nails into my ear, of course." He lifted his nose off the ground, considering. "I wouldn't try digging nails into me, if I were you."

Fredle clambered onto the nose and ran up between the raccoon's eyes to take shelter behind one bristly round ear. When he had a good hold, with all four paws, he asked, "What makes you think I'm so young?"

"Woo-Hah" was the only answer he got. With a ground-eating, loping run, Rilf headed off.

He went *that* way along the stone wall and when the break came, he turned onto the rutted road that sloped downward. After a while, he left the road and crossed a wide, overgrown field in those same long strides. At last he stopped and lowered his head.

Fredle had been trying to simultaneously hold on—but not with his nails—and remember the route, while all the time bouncing around on the raccoon's hard head, in danger of falling off at any moment. The sudden stop surprised him.

"Come *on*, Fredle." Rilf hurried him along. "Get down."

Fredle crawled shakily onto the ground, where the grass grew tall. "Where—" he started to ask, but he knew. Among all the other smells, he recognized the answer to his question: *Water*. Rilf had already buried his snout in water that was passing between two low banks right in front of them, rushing by—from where Fredle had no idea, and neither did he know where it was going. Although, just before he took his first taste, he almost remembered something. But then he had a mouth full of cold liquid, and was swallowing it, and he only thought about how good it was to drink.

After a while, he lifted his nose out of the water. "Thank you, Captain Rilf."

"Don't call me that, mouse. I'm not your captain. You're not one of the Rowdy Boys and you never will be."

"But— You said— Last night . . ."

"Yes?" Rilf growled.

"Sorry about that," Fredle said. This wasn't a quarrel he wanted to have. "It's just— I feel much better. I *was* thirsty."

"Plain Rilf will do, between a mouse and a raccoon."

Fredle nodded and said no more. He didn't need to understand raccoons. He just needed to get away from them.

As the light faded out of the air, Rilf turned his attention to a tall plant. He scratched at the base with his strong paws and then pulled something up out of the earth, letting it fall onto the ground. "You take this one, I'll get more."

Fredle looked at the thing. Its end was whitish and not large; its long leaves were green. He smelled it and it smelled like dirt, but something else, too. "What is it?"

"Try it, it's food. It's not poisonous. Well, not to raccoons, at least. We're about to find out about mice."

Fredle *was* hungry and he did need food of some kind. Rilf pulled up several more of the tall things and then took one himself. He reached down to put it into the water and rub it between his paws. Then he lifted the long, dripping thing up into the air to cram it—white bottom, long stem, leaves and all—into his mouth.

Fredle didn't see any other choice. He bit into the white end. It was crisp like apple peel but fresher than any apple peel or core from the compost. It was not sweet, not really; its flavor was sharp and it tasted good in a way Fredle had never tasted before. He took another bite.

"Ramps," said Rilf, taking up another and once again washing it in the water that flowed so quickly by them. "The stream grows watercress, too, but that's too bitter for me." He reached a paw down into the water to pull out something limp and dark green and leafy. "A mouse might like it."

"Should I wash this ramp before I eat it?" Fredle was trying on the new word, to be sure he'd gotten it right. He wasn't interested in watercress, whatever that was. "Should I be washing it in the stream, like you do?"

"It's too late now. Besides, I don't know why I do. A little dirt never hurt anyone, but if there's water and I've got something to eat, I wash it. Go figure. Finished with that one? Good, have one more and I will, too, and the rest I'll take back to the boys. I like to surprise them every now and then. It's one of the things a good captain does, if he wants to stay on top."

"But won't they be off foraging by now?"

"Maybe. Could be. Depending. But I bet we find them waiting."

"Where do they think you've gone?"

"Woo-Hah," Rilf laughed. "My guess is they think I'm off eating you on my own. That's a captain's privilege. Of course, a smart captain never takes advantage of his privileges, I can tell you that, my mouse. But as captain, I can eat what I want when I want it. As long as they're not hungry. And we all know they have that chicken carcass."

"If they don't forage, will they eat me instead?"

"They'll think about it. They'll want to. But all a raccoon needs to start him off at night is enough food to get him going. The chicken will do that. We'll have fresh ramps for after, if we want. Hop back on, young Fredle. We know your name," he said as Fredle made his careful way up the long snout and between the dark eyes. "So unless we haven't had anything to eat for a while, I'd say you're safe enough. For the time being. If the weather holds."

Fredle gripped an ear and thought about all this. He reminded himself of the appearance and the taste of the food Rilf had shown him, ramps, and the watercress the captain had pulled out of the stream. You never knew when you might need to know something. Rilf gathered up a mouthful of the long stalks and then he and Fredle were off again, heading through grainy darkness toward the burrow.

Rilf was proved correct. Three raccoons were waiting in the clearing when he came loping back. "We saved you the backbone, Cap'n."

Rilf lowered his head and let Fredle scramble off to retreat to the shelter of the wall. Then he emptied his mouth of its burden. "Ramps," he announced. "Dig in, boys. Or save them for tomorrow night. Whatever."

"I could use another mouthful," said Rec, but the others shouted him down: "Paws off! You're always trying to eat more. Give it a rest, Rec."

"What about the mouse, Cap'n?" asked Rad. "You want to kill him before we go? We don't want him running off on us."

Rilf waited too long for Fredle's comfort, as if he was thinking this over, but at last he said, "Fredle won't run off. He knows he can't find his way. Don't you, young Fredle?"

"Yes," Fredle answered, because it was true. He'd tried to run away, and failed.

"You don't believe that *inedible* stuff, do you, Cap'n?" asked Rec.

"What do you think?" Rilf answered.

"But what'll he eat? Because we don't want him starved and skinny. There's little enough meat on a mouse when he's fat," Rimble pointed out.

"He'll eat whatever we bring him." Rilf turned to Fredle. "Anything you want from the compost?"

This was not what Fredle had expected and it took him a few seconds to think of . . . "Apple peels?"

"Apple peels! Didja hear that?" And they were off again, laughing at him. "Woo-Hah, listen to that mouse, he wants us to bring apple peels back for him."

"I have to say, he's almost too much fun to eat," Rimble remarked.

"What's so funny?" demanded Fredle. "What's so funny about being hungry and wanting something good to eat?"

"What's so funny, young Fredle, is that if you climb over this stone wall you will find yourself in the middle of a whole field of apple trees. With apples lying scattered on the ground around them. A little rotten, maybe, after the winter cold, but apples all the same, enough to feed seven times seven herds of mice."

"What are they doing there?" asked Fredle. "Didn't Mister and Missus want them?"

"Nobody harvests these apples," Rilf told him. "It's as if nobody knows they're there. Deer eat them, and we do, too, if there's nothing better on offer. But raccoons are carnivores, basically. That means we eat meat, in case you don't know. Which includes mouse," he added.

"Includes Fredle the inedible, Woo-Hah," laughed Rec. "Can we get going? There's no garbage can for us tonight, I'm thinking, but what do you say to a good sniff around that chicken pen?"

"Who said you could give orders?" growled Rad. "You're not my captain."

"Can't we just *go*?" demanded Rimble.

"Happy foraging, Fredle," Rilf called back as the four raccoons lolloped off, leaving him alone in the night.

For a long time Fredle sat in the clearing in front of the wide-mouthed raccoon burrow. The air darkened around him. The black, shadowy branches of trees swayed in the wind, high around him. From where he sat, he could look up and see thin clouds that had stretched themselves across the sky. Through them he caught glimpses of stars, and then one of the smaller moons appeared, curved like an apple peel, and bright white. Hungry as he was, Fredle sat for a long time, looking up. As always, the stars comforted him. He should do something about being hungry, he knew, but he didn't move, looking at the stars and this moon, thinking about everything he had learned that day, remembering the stream—what was it he'd forgotten about streams?—and what Rilf had told him, about setting off in the right direction the first time, the direction of morning light, downhill. The clouds drifted off, leaving the stars and moon bright in the sky. Still, Fredle didn't move.

After a long while, however, he started to get curious

about those apples, over the wall. He scrambled awkwardly up over first one large stone, then another, then a third—jumping over the deep cracks where the stones did not fit together—until he stood on top.

From there he could see a dark expanse of star-strewn sky, beneath which he made out the shapes of many trees, standing in rows like the flowers at the front of the house. What would make those trees grow in rows? he wondered. The humans, probably. Only humans made such straight lines out of things, in flower beds, in the walls of a house, and even out in the wild, apparently, far from their homes.

These trees were smaller versions of the tall trees near the house, where squirrels lived. These trees had slender trunks and their branches didn't spread out so high above the ground. Pieces of white clouds were caught in their branches and there was a faint perfume in the air, like that of the flowers—although not exactly like it. Also in the air, now that Fredle paid attention to what he was smelling, he caught the scent of apples.

Careful not to go so fast that he lost footing, Fredle clambered down the other side of the stone wall. Back on the ground, the apple smell was stronger and the grass sparse, so he ran quickly to the nearest tree.

It stood among thin stalks of grass and a scattering of round, brown apples. Why were some apples dark gray, like the peels on the compost heap, while these were brown? Fredle wondered as he bit into one. This brown apple was softer, too, not at all crisp. It was as if this brown apple had soaked in water as it lay in the grass. But it tasted apple-y good, it filled his stomach, and when he finished eating it, he decided to take the core back with him, to his own tiny burrow in the wall. He had seen how Rilf carried ramps. With an apple core in his teeth, Fredle found that going over the stone wall was more difficult, but he managed it, tumbling back onto the ground at almost the exact same spot from which he had first started his

climb. Why, he asked himself as he drifted off to sleep, would humans keep their apple trees so far from the house, when the garden and the barn and the chickens and cats and dogs were kept so close?

The raccoons woke him when they returned, noisily

recounting their adventures of the evening to one another, boasting about taking a swat at an owl—"Thought I was some easy prey of a weasel but I showed him different!"—and facing down a rat—"They think they're the only ones with any rights to the grain bins. Woo-Hah. They think they've got the only sharp teeth on the farm."

"We brought a couple of corncobs," Rimble told Fredle.

"He's got a whole field of apples," Rec objected.

"We share," Rilf told them. "That's how the Rowdy Boys do it. There's enough for all of us, and besides, if ordinary mouse is tasty, a fat, corn-fed mouse will be even tastier."

"Right you are, Cap'n," they said.

"Actually, thank you, but I'm not hungry," Fredle told them. They made him nervous. The idea of eating with them made him even more nervous.

"Woo-Hah," they laughed.

"If you'd ever had corn," Rec advised him, entirely serious, "you wouldn't miss the chance to have it again."

The raccoons weren't ready to sleep. It wasn't light yet and they were still excited by the night's adventures.

"Those dogs never even suspected we were there."

"I'd have brought you an egg," Rilf told Fredle, "but they don't transport well, too fragile. I'd have ended up with a mouthful of shell."

"Ick-ko," agreed Rimble.

"You are such a coonlet," Rec said.

Rimble snapped at the big raccoon, teeth flashing. "I'll show you coonlet and I'll take off some of your fat while I'm at it."

The two snarled at one another until Rad interrupted to

report, "Things are looking promising in the garden, Cap'n. She's planted lettuce, and the peas and peppers are already sprouted."

"Rain tomorrow," predicted Rilf. When the other raccoons groaned at the news, "Don't be so soft," he told them. "How do you feel about rain, young Fredle?"

"Young Inedible," said Rec.

"Young Incredible," added Rimble.

"Woo-Hah," they laughed.

"I don't mind rain. It means good drinking," Fredle said.

"Who wants to have to live off rainwater? Not us." The Rowdy Boys all agreed on this point. "We've got the stream and we've got the lake, too. When do we move to the lake, Cap'n? It's warm enough, isn't it? Winter's well gone. Which do you think tastes better," they asked one another, "fresh fish or fresh mouse?"

"When do we go up to the summer burrow, Cap'n?" they asked again, and more eagerly.

Once again, Fredle was distracted by something he couldn't remember about that stream. The forgotten thing chittered like a chicken at the edge of his mind.

"The girls will be wanting to see us, and show off their coonlets."

Rilf looked at Fredle and then at the Rowdy Boys. He looked up into the air and then back at Fredle. He was watching Fredle when he answered, "We'll be there in time for the full moon."

"Not long, then," Rec observed, and he, too, looked at Fredle.

"I'm almost sorry," said Rad, staring as well at the mouse in their midst.

Fredle guessed he knew what they were thinking of. "Me too," he agreed.

"Woo-Hah," they all laughed.

He didn't join in.

13

The Moon's Story

Fredle thought very carefully about the situation; he didn't want to make mistakes because of being frightened, or hungry, or just plain impatient. The first thing he needed to know, if it was something that could be known, was: How long did he have before a full moon appeared in the night sky? As far as Fredle had seen, the different moons appeared at random out of the darkness and sometimes there was no moon at all. But maybe raccoons knew something he didn't about moons. Maybe raccoons had lived in the wild long enough to understand what was going on in the sky as well as mice understood what was going on in the kitchen. Fredle needed to find out what the raccoons knew, without making Rilf suspicious.

He couldn't spend too many hours thinking about all of this, either, because who knew when some full moon would take it into its head to pop up in the sky, and that would be the end of him.

That evening, when the raccoons woke up and were having a snack of stale chocolate cake, they offered some to Fredle. He recognized the smell. "Mice can't eat chocolate," he told them.

"Poor you," said Rec, but didn't sound sorry at the prospect of increasing his own share even by one-quarter of the small amount a mouse would eat.

"It's really good, Fredle," said Rimble, who didn't have many chances to be the raccoon picking on someone. "It's sweet. Smell it. It can't hurt you just to smell it, can it?"

Fredle turned his back on them and looked up at the sky, where only one star shone, low in the purple darkness of evening. He studied it for a long time, as the raccoons slurped and swallowed behind him, before asking, carelessly, without even turning around, "Is that one of the moons up there? Over the apple trees?"

"What do you mean, *one* of the moons?" asked Rad.

"Did you hear what he said?" Rimble asked. "That mouse can't tell the moon from a moonbit."

"Woo-Hah, stupid mouse," laughed Rec.

"Unless— Do you think he's making fun of us?" asked Rimble. "Because if he is— What do you think, Rec, do we let the mouse get away with that?"

"He could be," said Rec, menacingly. "I think he might need to be taught a lesson."

"And we're the ones to teach him," Rimble agreed.

"If you two are looking for a fight, why not pick on someone your own size?" asked Rad. "Like me, for instance." He growled low in his throat. Rec snarled, showing his teeth. Fredle moved back toward the shelter of the stone wall, in case one of their fights broke out.

But Rilf interrupted. "Is that right, Fredle?" he asked. "No one ever told you about moonbits?"

"I'm a house mouse," Fredle said. He wanted badly to tell those raccoons everything he knew about the moons that came out among what he *knew* humans called stars. However, his plan was to not be eaten, which was more important than showing off how smart he was.

"Makes sense, then, that he wouldn't know, doesn't it, Cap'n?" asked Rad. "Being that house mice live inside. These two stupids wouldn't have the imagination to figure that out. You should tell the mouse the story."

"What story?" asked Rimble. "You mean the moon story?"

"I thought we were heading out, to forage," protested Rec.

"There's all night for that," Rilf told him, and turned to Fredle. "That little bright thing you asked about, the one that looks like it's tangled up in those tree branches? That's a moonbit. There are moonbits all over the sky but you can only see them at night when the air is dark. During daylight they blend in with the air, because they're so pale. Those moonbits used to be part of the moon, way back. Way back, when the moon was young and just starting to grow, the way young things do, way back then, the raccoons *wanted* the moon to get bigger. When there were none of those big gray sky-leaves covering him, the moon gave out a bright light for raccoons. We could see everything clearly, mice in the fields, squirrels running over tree roots, fish in the lake, ramps and dande-lions." Rilf broke off and remarked to Fredle, "I bet you don't know what a lake is."

"Or a fish," Fredle agreed.

"You curious?" Rilf asked.

Fredle nodded.

"The lake's water that's always there. Some summers the banks and beaches get wider, but it never dries up. In fact, it keeps filling up, we know it has to, because there's a stream always running out of it, down the side of the mountain to land up nobody knows where. But the stream doesn't matter because there are no fish in it."

"There are frogs in the stream, Cap'n," said Rad. "Frog is good. Better than mouse."

"There's not enough meat on a frog. Give me a plump mouse anytime, especially a plump house mouse," Rec said. "Mouse is better than squirrel, too, because they don't have all that fur. Fur—ick-ko."

"I see you're bored with the story," Rilf said crossly.

"No, Cap'n, not a bit of it," Rec answered quickly. "Or anyway, *I'm* not. You two, snap shut. And you"—he turned to Fredle—"no questions. Understood?"

Fredle wasn't about to answer. It was the frogs that did it. Those frogs reminded him of what it was he'd been trying to think of, ever since Rilf took him across the field to eat ramps and drink water—from the stream! He remembered hearing Sadie's voice saying something. But he couldn't remember *what* it was he'd heard.

Rilf went on with the story, and now there were two

things Fredle was paying close attention to, both at the same time: the full moon question and the stream-Sadie memory. He took a deep breath, looking straight at Rilf. *I can do this*, he thought.

"For a long time," Rilf was saying, "the raccoons left food out for the moon, all the things the moon likes, fish bones and chicken bones, grassy stalks, eggshells, apple cores, too. The moon has a real taste for apple cores. The moon ate everything and grew bigger, and bigger, and bigger. He grew so big the raccoons began to get worried. Do you want to know why, young Fredle?" he asked.

Fredle nodded. He could think about two things at the same time, but he couldn't talk as well. Three was too many for him.

"The moon was grown so big, it was starting to crowd down from the sky onto their territory. The raccoons were afraid that before long that moon would either crush them or crowd them back into corners where nothing grew and no prey lived. After that, they knew, it wouldn't be very long before there were no raccoons left at all. But what could they do?"

"They could stop feeding him," Fredle suggested, unable to stop himself.

"Wow, Fredle, that's a really good idea," Rimble said, in a sarcastic voice. "Like it wasn't already way too late for that."

Rilf ignored both of them. He went on with his story. "What they did was gather together the wisest and strongest raccoons. To talk about ways to get rid of the moon, all the wisest and strongest raccoons, each one cleverer than the last—because raccoons are famous for being clever. Even mice know that, right, Fredle? But that big fat moon was right there, always, listening in on everything they said."

He waited, to let them consider that problem.

In the silence, Fredle remembered: Sadie had said she wanted to run over to the stream for a drink of water, that it was close by, but she couldn't go because she had her job of watching the baby. He remembered being in the garden and Sadie saying that to him. He almost melted into the dirt with relief.

"They did stop feeding the moon and they totally ignored him, hoping that he would go away to another sky. But the monstrous thing hung around. Getting bigger. Not getting bigger as fast as he had, but still . . . Things were dire, you can imagine. Until finally they had an idea. Just one hope, the only plan they could think of."

"It was a *great* plan," Rad told Fredle. "If it hadn't been for them, we wouldn't be here today."

Fredle wasn't sure that would be such a terrible thing, but he certainly didn't say that out loud. He was being careful to pay close attention to Rilf's story so as not to give away his excitement at what he had just remembered. He asked, "What was the plan? How could raccoons stop the moon?"

"I said no questions," growled Rec.

Rilf's voice grew proud. "Way back then, there was a raccoon living who was bigger and stronger, and therefore wiser, too, seven times bigger and stronger and wiser than the biggest and strongest and wisest raccoon that has ever lived. His name was Rasta and he would have made even Rec look scrawny and thin."

"Woo-Hah," laughed Rimble.

"Rasta had long, clawed paws that could break boulders, and he was brave, too. Raccoons are always brave—"

"You better believe it," said Rad.

"—but Rasta was seven times as brave as any other raccoon has ever been. So when the moon came shining down the way he liked to in those days, so bright you had to shut your eyes tight not to be blinded by him, Rasta was waiting. The moon sank his great belly down into the cool lake and Rasta grabbed onto that fat white moon with one paw."

Rilf demonstrated this by holding one arm out to the side.

"With the other"—Rilf gestured with his other arm, acting out the story—"he tore into him, as if the moon was no more than just any old fish or other food. Rasta tore off bits and pieces of that moon, and he tossed them aside, up into the air."

"And those are the moonbits," Rimble announced to Fredle, "and that's why there are so many of them. So now you know."

"Let Cap'n finish," Rad said.

"I was only saying," Rimble complained.

Rilf raised his voice over this quarreling. "The moon tried to get free. He twisted and turned, rolled backward and forward, but Rasta held him tight. The moon tried to escape the paw that was shredding him to bits, and the claw that was holding him; he howled and he cursed, but Rasta didn't let go. It was hard work, long work, but Rasta kept at it, for seven nights and seven days, too. He didn't rest, he didn't sleep, he didn't eat. And gradually, slowly, the moon weakened, and shrank, and got pale."

"What about all the other moons?" asked Fredle. "The ones that aren't full moons? Why didn't they come to save him?"

"There's only ever been one moon, young Fredle," Rilf told him.

Fredle wasn't so sure about that. He wasn't sure about anything he was being told, but he didn't say so to the raccoons. He wasn't about to say to them, *Don't try to fool me about moons, I've seen them.* Whatever he said now needed to have only one purpose: to find out when the full moon was going to come out in the sky, so he could know how much time he had. "Then what happened?" he asked.

"Then that moon started begging Rasta to stop. 'What'll you do for light without me?' he asked, but Rasta didn't answer. 'All I wanted to do was grow,' he said, but Rasta said not a word, just kept taking off moonbits and tossing them off into the darkness. Until at last the moon said, 'All right, I give up, I'll stop.'

"By then, he was no bigger than he'd been to start out. 'Promise,' said Rasta, and 'I promise,' the moon said. But Rasta knew what a liar and trickster that moon was. Do you know what he did then?"

"Kept on ripping pieces off?" Fredle guessed.

"Nope."

"Tied a string to him so he couldn't get away?"

"Nope."

Fredle thought. "Climbed onto him and stayed there, ready to attack again?"

"Nope and nope," Rilf said. "Rasta was smarter than that, and way smarter than you, smarter than even me. Rasta figured that if the moon liked growing, that was the way to make his promise stick. He told the moon that in order for Rasta, and all raccoons in all the time to come, to be sure the moon was keeping his promise, the moon would have to grow smaller first, and after that he could grow bigger again, but then he'd have to grow smaller again so he could grow bigger, over and over. As long as the moon did that, he could have the sky safe to himself. Which is what the moon has done, ever since. Raccoons know there's only one moon, because we keep an eye on him. We'd know if another moon showed up, to start making trouble again. The moon watches us, too, hoping we'll forget, or get bored and go away somewhere else. We're the ones that keep him where he belongs. If he didn't see us watching, ready to call up Rasta to turn him into nothing but moonbits forever, I don't know what that moon might get up to."

"Is Rasta still alive?" asked Fredle, curious despite not believing that the story could be true.

"The moon is growing now," Rimble announced. "He's about half-size, at least. Wouldn't you say half-size, Cap'n? So when do we leave for the lake?" He turned to Fredle. "It takes three nights' heavy traveling to get there."

"Maybe tomorrow, maybe the night after," Rilf said. "It won't be long. I can promise you that. Fredle's never seen a lake, and he's never seen the way the moon lays out a silver road on the water."

Water big enough to have a road on it? A road the color of moonlight? Fredle wondered what that might look like, and he almost asked. But Rilf was still talking, and besides, Fredle realized, if he was lucky he'd never find out.

"The mouse has to see that before we eat him," Rilf went on. "And he has to eat fish, too. That's what I say." He looked around at the Rowdy Boys. "Anybody want to argue?"

Fredle did, but he kept quiet, thinking about how he might escape, and when. He was going to have to try it soon, probably right away. That much he had understood clearly from Rilf's story. That part of the story he completely believed.

He also understood, from having lived among the raccoons, that one chance was all he would get. If they knew he was thinking of escaping, and depriving them of their long-anticipated treat, they'd finish him off immediately and even Rilf would agree that that was the best thing to do. In fact, it was probably only thanks to Rilf that Fredle hadn't went that first night, and he knew, as surely as he knew himself to be perfectly edible, that he couldn't count on Rilf's interest for much longer. Fredle was a diversion for the Rowdy Boys; he gave them something new to quarrel about, which made Rilf's job easier. But that wasn't going to last much longer. Fredle understood that, too.

"When are we leaving, Cap'n?" they asked, and Rilf answered, "Soon. Very soon. Trust me."

"We do, Cap'n," they answered. "Never doubt it."

"I'm wondering how many of the coonlets survived the winter," Rilf said. "Two of them looked too weak, but you never know; maybe they didn't have to give them to the foxes after all."

"Not likely," Rad remarked. "There's always a couple of coonlets that have to go."

"Lucky for me I wasn't one of those," said Rimble. "Neither were none of us and especially not old fatso here. *He* was never too scrawny and weak to spend good food on."

"Woo-Hah," they laughed, and Rec laughed with them. "Anybody else hungry?"

14

Escape

After the raccoons went off to raid the chicken pen and the barn, Fredle made his decision: he would head out the next morning. For a solitary mouse, traveling in the wild, outside, day might be a safer time than night—or so he hoped. Also, whereas the raccoons might return at any time during the night, depending on how their foraging went, they could be counted on to sleep most of the day.

So he knew *when* he was going. He also knew *where*. He would go *that* way along the stone wall until he came to the break, and then he would turn toward the brightening sky and go along the dirt road until he came to the field, and then he would turn into the field—also *that* way. His shoulders remembered the direction. Crossing the field to get to the stream would be the most dangerous part of the journey, he guessed. It was easy for Rilf, with his long legs and loping stride, but not for Fredle, who was a short-legged scurrier. Fredle would just have to keep on going until he came to the stream.

And after that?

After that, he hoped that he would be able to follow the stream back to where the garden might be near. He hoped he would know when he'd followed it far enough, but not too far. But how could he know that?

In any case, Fredle would need to be well fed and well rested before starting off, so he crossed over the wall and ate more than his fill of the apples lying on the ground. Then he returned to his usual sleeping place, sheltered within the stone wall. He didn't expect to sleep much, or easily, or deeply, but he did. He didn't even wake up when the raccoons came home. In fact, Rilf had to poke him awake to offer him a section of potato peel.

Fredle ate it as if he were hungry and then pretended to go back to sleep, while he waited for the raccoons to settle down.

The air lightened and a soft rain started to fall, while Fredle listened for the snoring to begin and thought about traveling in the rain. It was less comfortable for him, that was for sure; on the other hand, the raccoons would be less likely to stir from the comfort of their burrow and discover that he was gone. On the whole, he decided, he would count it as good luck that rain came on the morning he had decided to make his escape.

Soon enough he heard four raccoons snoring almost in unison, and knew it was time. But now that he was about to actually take the first steps, he felt reluctant to leave behind something he knew and go out into who knew what landscape, into who knew what future. He began to worry that he had made an error in remembering what Sadie said, and to wonder if the stream Rilf took him to was really the same stream Sadie had wanted to drink from. Then he reminded himself that his other choice was to be a raccoon dinner in not very many nights. He reminded himself that if he waited much longer, the Rowdy Boys would carry him even farther away from the house, from home, making it even less likely that he would ever find his way back.

This was his chance, and he knew it. He wanted to take it, too. So he did.

Fredle did not look back but moved off as quietly as only a mouse can in *that* direction, staying close to the stone wall, where there were many openings into which a mouse could squeeze himself, to hide. He was so frightened and excited that he barely noticed the rain. This was a gentle, steady rain that coated the stones and moistened the dirt beneath his paws. It shone on the blades of grass through which Fredle moved as rapidly as he could, escaping.

He came to the break in the wall what felt like a long time later, although he knew that was only in comparison to how quickly he had made the trip riding behind Rilf's ear. He did not allow himself to rest at the break but turned immediately onto the rutted road. His shoulders remembered the direction Rilf had taken to get to the stream, *that* way again, but he had no sense of how far he should go before turning off.

As he scrambled along, the rain stopped and Fredle found the going easier. He could plan ahead then: At the stream, if he could get there, he could forage for ramps and maybe even that dark green watercress Rilf had pointed out. At the stream, if he could find it, he could drink water. And somewhere downstream, Sadie had said, he would be near the garden, and the house.

Near for a dog with her long legs, Fredle reminded himself. He wondered who moved faster, a raccoon or a dog. He knew who covered distances more slowly and with more difficulty— a mouse. But just because you didn't move fast didn't mean you wouldn't arrive. You would just arrive later and later wasn't such a big deal, especially compared to never.

Fredle hurried along the rough terrain, stopping to sip water out of puddles when he grew too thirsty not to. The day went on. When he judged—how could he know? he could only guess—that he had gone far enough, he turned *that* way for the third time, as Rilf had done, and scrambled up onto the field.

While he knew the direction he wanted, he didn't know what dangers might be hunting for him in the long grass, or catch sight of him as they flew through the air above. He would be safest among the thickest clumps of grass, he thought, so he made his cautious way from one thick cluster to the next, dashing between them, stopping to catch his breath and listen for danger. Above him, the air still had light, but it was a gray and sunless brightness. He didn't know how much of the day was left.

He hoped he wouldn't have to sleep unsheltered, unhidden, unprotected. He also hoped he wouldn't have to cross too much of the field at night. It was with dread that Fredle saw light fading around him and knew that he could not even *hear* the stream. Day was ending. Night was coming on. Fredle's fears grew.

If, he thought anxiously, if he had left the road too soon, he would never come to the stream, but would wander lost in the field until some predator finished him off. Or maybe he had turned off too late, so the stream lay behind him and he would wander lost in the field until some predator finished him off. Either of those misfortunes was possible; Fredle understood that. But the only thing he could do was go on.

Darkness and exhaustion caught up with him. How far across the field he might have gotten, Fredle couldn't know. He might have been only ten steps from the stream—although he doubted that, since he could neither hear nor smell water. But he had come to a point—and also to a thick tuft of tall grass—where he could go no farther. He curled himself up on the ground at the foot of the stalks to rest, to sleep.

Neither the stars nor a moon could be seen, only low clouds.

Maybe, he thought hopefully, he was difficult to see in whatever shelter the grass was giving him, in the darkness.

Tired as he was, he was not so deeply asleep that rain didn't wake him when it began falling again, pattering onto the stalks around him. He awoke cold and, of course, wet. He rose unhappily to his feet and drank some of the rainwater that was weighing down the long blades of grass. Then he set off again, going through more darkness. The air was thick with falling rain, and lightless. Fredle could hear nothing except the sound of rain hitting the ground. The sky overhead was dark, the field all around him more densely dark and filled with moving shapes. The only color was the occasional silver glint of rain, falling.

He didn't allow himself to wonder what the coming day would bring. He just set off in the direction that felt right to his shoulders. He set off and kept going.

A lightening in the air told him when day began, which was good news. Still, he could see only rain and wet grass. He trudged on and on and then—all unready—he had come to water. He heard a gurgling sound behind the pattering of rain. He smelled a change in the watery odor of the air. He lifted his eyes from the place where he planned to place his front paws for the next step and saw that he stood on the bank of the stream.

In fact, Fredle was so surprised that he almost slid down into the water, what with the wet soil and the slippery grass of the bank; he just managed to save himself.

Standing on the bank, the water rushing by below him, the rain falling down on him from above, Fredle felt like giving a cheer. "Woo-Hah!" he laughed, as wild as any raccoon. He had done it! "Woo-Hah!" He was still wet and cold, he was still hungry and tired, but he had found the stream. Maybe, as the day went on, the rain would stop and there would be sunlight and the sunlight would warm him and dry him. He hoped so. In the meantime, he set about finding one of the ramp plants, and digging it up, and eating it. The ramp tasted so good that he set about digging up another, and then—he didn't think he'd ever been so hungry in his life—he rooted around among the stalks of grass at the steep side of the stream for a third.

That was when he lost his footing. He scrabbled at the dirt with his rear paws, with his front paws, desperately seeking

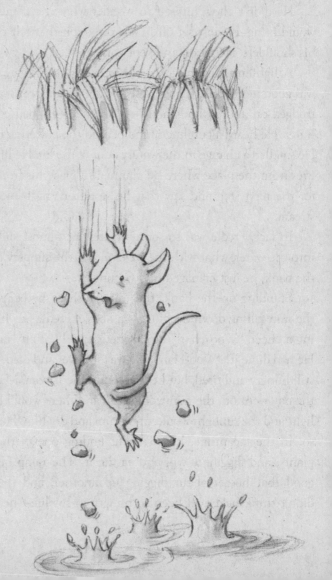

some kind of grip as he started to slip down the bank. He was still struggling when the water closed over his head.

Fredle gasped—it was so cold! When he gasped his mouth filled and he wanted to cough but he couldn't because his throat was full. There was water all around him. His feet searched, but he was upside down until the current flipped him over and he felt something solid underfoot and without even thinking—he could no more think than swim—he pushed against it, pushed hard, to escape back up into the air, where he would be able to breathe. The water was flowing past him and dragging him along.

His head broke the surface and then he could cough, while the fast-moving stream shoved him back toward the same bank he had fallen from, although a good distance down from the spot where he had lost his footing. Fredle snatched at a narrow root that stuck out from the side and clung to it, until he had the strength to pull himself up onto it. Hanging over it, he coughed until at last he could breathe easily again. He shivered, until he shivered himself warm. Only a pale early-morning light was in the air. He looked up through the rain to see how he could get back up to the field. Here, although the bank was steeper, he thought he *might* be able to scramble up, grasping grasses and roots, as soon as he had his strength back. The bank curved in behind his root, just slightly, as if the moving water had washed away some soil, making a small burrow. That was what had bared the root that saved him. But it was also something that might make it harder for him to get back to the ground because it made an overhang, right above him.

Cautiously, he turned his head and was relieved to see that

the soil behind him held a rock too large to be swept away by the rushing water. If he could turn himself around without falling back into the water, he would have an easy climb out.

He hoisted himself up onto the root. Grateful for his mouse's good sense of balance and light weight, he rotated— slowly, slowly—careful to grip the moist bark with his nails. By now, the rain was reduced to a fine spray and the air was brightening. Fredle paid no attention to rain or light but concentrated fiercely on the task before him.

Their voices took him entirely by surprise.

Fredle froze.

Then he wondered if he should do what outside mice did and make a dash for it. But that would mean leaping into the water, and he thought his best hope lay in stillness. He didn't move. He barely breathed.

Rilf said, "I can't get a whiff of him anymore. Can you?"

"I can't, Cap'n," Rad answered. "The boys are none too pleased. You think we should have gone right after him last night?"

"With all that food in our bellies? Besides, how was I to know he wasn't off in the orchard, stuffing his face," Rilf's voice said. "Then the rain. It was bad enough without the rain watering up his scent," he grumbled.

"You know, Cap'n, if you think about it, we don't *have* to go back. Not you and me. We could go straight on to the lake. Those two will never find the lake on their own and we'd never have to see them again."

"My guess is, he fell in. What do you think, could he fall in?"

"Drowned, then?"

"And the body washed up who knows how far downstream. Too far for us to retrieve him. I didn't think he'd do this to me."

"In all fairness, Cap'n, we *were* going to eat him. You can't really blame him."

Then Rilf laughed, "Woo-Hah. You've got the right of it, Rad. I could almost admire that mouse."

"So, are we going to go back to the burrow?" asked Rad. "I have to say, I could use some sleep. I'm pretty worn out."

"We might just be going back to trouble," said Rilf, not unhappily, and Fredle was almost sure that he heard the nasal voice moving away. "A bit of trouble always cheers me up," Rilf said, his voice now faint.

After that, there was silence. It was not a complete silence, naturally. There was the rush of the stream and, with growing daylight, the voices of birds. Fredle waited on the root, resting. The sun came out and dried him and as he waited it also dried the dirt on the bank in front of him. He continued to wait, and rest.

If you will have only one chance, you want to make it the best it can be.

After a long time, Fredle reached out, cautiously, gently, to grab at the dirt with one front paw while digging the nails of the other into the top of the stone. With his two back paws still on the root, using all the strength in his haunches, he pushed himself off.

He scrabbled and clung, climbed over up onto the rock and stretched his front paws up, up, to the grassy edge of the bank. Then it was just a scramble up over the top until he could lie panting among the grass and overgrowth of the field. When he had caught his breath, he dug up a ramp, and then another, and ate them both.

By then the sun had thoroughly warmed the air and insects flew busily about. Fredle set off, following the fast-moving water, going downstream. He had no idea what waited for him next. The only idea he had was *home*.

15

Downstream

Fredle did not rush the journey. He knew better than to exhaust himself by trying to race over rough ground. As he traveled along the bank of the stream, stopping to eat ramps when he was hungry, to sleep in the best protection he could find when he was tired, he enjoyed all the scents of the field and stream, the calls of the birds and the humming of insects, the blue or gray of the sky, the green of the grass, and even the blackness of crows. At night, although he could not enjoy the screeching of raptors or the cries of their victims, he could see the stars and moons. The night a full moon shone in the sky, Fredle stayed still for a long time, watching, while the silvered stream whispered beside him. Had he been lucky? Or had he been brave? Or only clever? A little of all three, he decided, staring at the flat white circle whose light made darker shadows than the sun ever did. Fredle wondered if there really was only one moon—but how could it change itself? That would be as if Fredle could shrink from a whole mouse to, for example, half a mouse and then just a mouse tail, and then could grow back to being his entire self again and after that—strangest of all—diminish again.

But was that any more improbable than several different moons appearing only one at a time? Fredle watched and wondered.

Although it was the more dangerous time for a mouse out in the wild, Fredle preferred traveling by night, with the stars so beautiful overhead and the shadows all around so mysterious. He was the most anxious and afraid traveling by night, but also the most awake.

He trudged on and on. He grew tired of the taste of ramps, and of the bitter green watercress leaves, too. He wondered if there were other wild plants a mouse might eat, but didn't want to risk trying what others hadn't assured him was safe. Others were not always right and they were not always wrong; they didn't always know what was true and they didn't always tell the truth. But Fredle had come to prefer first listening to what others had to say and then deciding for himself. He would, he thought, be an easier mouse to get along with when he got back home.

One afternoon, he knew. He breathed in, and knew. He had been scrambling along the side of the stream, listening to the contented watery gurgling beside him, the sharp cries of crows, and then, unexpectedly, unquestioningly, he knew.

Home was off *this* way. He could hear nothing familiar, could see nothing familiar, but he knew. He turned in *this* direction, entering a field. These tall stalks were not grass. They were higher and narrower and not as green as grass. He didn't know what they were, but they were the way home.

It was a good thing he was sure of his direction, because with the dense stalks waving over his head as well as slowing his progress, he had no way to see what lay ahead. The day wore on and Fredle was both thirsty and hungry, but he did not stop. There was, after all, nothing to drink and nothing to eat there in that field.

He came to its end and peered ahead, and recognized the dark gray mass of the barn up ahead. A wide, muddy patch of ground with fence poles along it lay between him and the barn, but that didn't bother him because he knew now *exactly* where he was. He skirted the fence, sticking close to whatever cover he could find, dashing from post to post and then scurrying in close to the wall of what he knew must be the woodshed.

Now he could begin to worry about those barn cats, and he did. Ahead of him lay the wide, grassy distance between woodshed and garden that he would have to cross in order to make his way back to the garbage cans, and the way in. The barn cats patrolled that area. If he was lucky, they wouldn't be patrolling it now. If he was unlucky . . .

Cautiously, Fredle rounded the corner by the open front of the woodshed. There he hesitated, trying to see in late-afternoon shadows if there were cats on the prowl. He saw nothing. He heard nothing from the woodshed mice. One of

the roaring machines roared into the barn and then fell abruptly silent. Fredle knew from experience that at the approach of one of those machines all creatures, even the dogs, retreated to shelter. So he judged that it was safe—or at least safe enough—to make a move. He took two small steps out from the protection of the woodshed wall.

The voice came from above him. "Slowly, slowly—a smart little mousie it is. That it is."

Fredle froze. He looked up.

The snake hung down from a ceiling beam, swaying in the shadows like the branch of one of the apple trees when a wind pulled at it. A tongue darted in and out of the snake's mouth. Its golden eyes shone.

"Lucky little mousie, too."

Fredle inched backward.

"Why lucky? Because I just finished eating. Maybe you knew my supper? Although I didn't catch the name." There was a hissing sound. Was that snake laughter? "I just caught the mousie."

Fredle inched another two steps back toward the wall. He couldn't look away from the glistening hooded eyes.

"Maybe," the snake said, as if the idea had just struck it, "it's just smart? If this little mousie had tried to run, I'd have had to catch it, and crush it. Any black rat snake

168

knows that rule. If it runs, you catch it, you crush it, you eat it if you're hungry. That's our way."

The snake swayed above and Fredle inched below. "Do you have instinct, too, little mousie?" the snake asked.

But Fredle had backed away out of sight and retreated around the corner of the woodshed. He stayed there, pressed up against the wall, until the shivers stopped running back and forth across his shoulders. He had a new respect for Neldo and Bardo. He didn't think he could manage to live so close to that long, black, hissing thing.

After that, and giving the open front of the woodshed a wide berth, Fredle moved without thinking, moved fast so as to be out of sight before the cats emerged from wherever they had fled to when the roaring machine entered the barn. This time he didn't look around to see whatever there was to be seen, and, hungry as he was, he didn't even *want* to stop in the grass by the chicken pen to see if the woodshed mice had missed any kernels of corn. He would much rather be hungry and thirsty than crushed in the coils of a snake or trapped under the claws of a cat. It wasn't until he had huddled up against the protection of a garden fence post that he allowed himself to think ahead, and even then he thought no farther ahead than his passage across the dirt road to the garbage cans.

He planned to be far away from those garbage cans and the compost before dark. It was unlikely that the raccoons would have returned from the lake, and its fish, so soon, but as Fredle had learned, *unlikely* was very different from *sure and certain*. For a mouse it was, anyway. So when he had rested enough to make another all-out run, Fredle just dashed off. He thought he could hear the dogs, barking, but not clearly enough to know what they were saying. He might have heard his name being called, but he wasn't about to be diverted. He ran at top speed, using all the strength and energy he had left.

Behind the big green containers he stopped again, to rest, but as soon as he could he crept around them to get to the foundation and its protecting bushes. He felt a strong urge to go in the opposite direction, *that* way—to return to his lattice wall and the solitary nest behind it—but he resisted, making himself turn *this* way. He followed the foundation, scrambling over the roots of the bushes and through their thick, tangled branches, until he came to the remembered window, with its cracked frame. Without a second's hesitation, he squeezed through and dropped down onto the dirt, where at last he could stop running.

Fredle was back inside.

16

In the Cellar

It was as he remembered it, a soft dirt floor and in the distance a faint glimmer of gray light. For a long time, Fredle sat where he was, glad to have made it, glad to feel the dry ground under him, glad to feel a ceiling even closer overhead than the ceiling over his territory under the porch, mostly just glad to have gotten safely back inside. After that long time, he began to make his way toward the light.

This was nothing like sun-filled daylight, or even the cold brightness of the moon. In fact, it was the dim kind of light he remembered from home. As he crossed the packed dirt, sometimes stumbling over a stone or a piece of wood, his eyes gradually grew accustomed and he saw that the brighter space ahead had the same shape as the windows in the foundation of the house.

Coming closer, he began to hear something. *Voices*, he thought, *and maybe even mouse voices*. But it couldn't be, and especially it couldn't be the voices of many mouselets, which was what it really sounded like. One of the first things a mouselet learned was to be silent, no matter what was making him unhappy, no matter how hungry or frightened or even excited he might feel. Any sound could attract the cat. These mouselet voices—and every now and then Fredle also heard an adult—were so abnormal it made him nervous. He tried to remember everything he had ever heard about the cellar mice.

They had to live on soap and string, he remembered, but that was all he knew. If they ate soap and string, they were probably as scrawny as any field mouse; probably he could escape easily from any one of them, although probably also he could fight his way free. He'd learned how to fight from watching the raccoons.

When he arrived at the window-shaped opening, which went through a thick stone-and-mortar wall just like the foundation, Fredle stopped, to get his bearings and to figure out what awaited him up ahead. He crept cautiously across the wall. The voices grew louder, clearer. They were not angry voices, and neither were they unhappy, and especially they weren't fearful.

"My turn now!"

"Roar, roar, I'm the cat!"

"Me, chase me!"

"I'm getting ready to spring! Freeze, mouselet!"

"You can't scare *me*, Mr. Cat."

"It's not her turn, it's mine!"

When kitchen mouselets played, they played in whispers, but if they had played out loud it might have sounded like this.

Fredle crept farther forward. He leaned out into the empty air, to smell, to hear, and even to see whatever there was to be seen. Then, unable to see anything yet, he leaned farther out.

He just had time to smell something—food?—before he tumbled down, off the stone-and-mortar wall, and fell into empty air.

There was nothing to grab on to, but luckily he thumped to a stop almost immediately and lay there, the breath knocked out of him.

He had landed on something hard, and smooth, and round. When he landed on it, it shifted underneath him and, instinctively, still struggling for breath, still recovering from the shock of his fall, he dug every one of his sharp little nails into it.

It was soft inside, and it smelled . . . like food, smelled almost like ramps, smelled so good he couldn't think of anything else and he certainly didn't notice that all the voices had been stilled by the sound of his fall.

Then he did notice it and grew worried. He saw that wherever it was he had fallen had high walls circling up all around him. He was on top of a mound of these round things—onions! He recognized them now. All around him rose a dark, curved wall, much higher, and much, much wider, than the sides of the ice cream container had been. He would never be able to climb up and out, although he was going to have to try.

He heard faint, faint sounds, the sounds of mice moving quietly, not far away. After that, silence fell again.

Could he go down rather than up? Fredle wondered. Could he make his way through these piled-up onions without getting trapped among them?

And what were all these onions doing here, anyway? Probably it was something that had to do with the humans. After all, it was their cellar, so anything in it would be something they put there.

Fredle decided that he *would* try moving down to escape, since he couldn't move up. He crawled over to the edge of the pile and discovered that the whatever-it-was was not made of thick, impenetrable plastic like the garbage containers, or of paper like the ice cream container, but of something between straw and wood, by the smell of it. If he had to, he knew, he could chew through wood or straw. However, before he tried eating his way out, he began to squeeze and squirm between the onions, moving toward the bottom of the pile. He wouldn't want to take all the time and trouble of chewing through, only to find himself so high above any ground that he would have no other choice but to leap out into empty space, and hope.

He made his way down around one of the onions, and another, and another, until he could feel them piled high above him, heavy. He didn't like to think about that, so he stopped himself from thinking about anything and squeezed himself down again, always staying close to the side of the whatever-it-was.

From below, a voice asked, "Mouse or foe?"

"Mouse," Fredle answered without thinking, and then he realized that that was just the way a cat, or a snake, might try to trick you.

"I don't know," said the voice, sounding now a little closer, and definitely mouselike. "You don't smell like mouse. You smell like onion."

"I'm no onion," Fredle said, and then he laughed. "Woo-Hah. What do you expect to smell, in all these onions? Apples?" But while he was laughing, he tried to position himself so that at least his front paws were free and his mouth was not blocked, so that if need be he could do some serious scratching and biting.

"Apples are in another basket," said the voice, which hadn't moved either closer or farther away. "Exit's down this way. Follow my voice."

What else could Fredle do? He crept toward the voice. It was very dark in among the onions—in the *basket*, he repeated to himself—and the spaces were tight, even for a mouse. He dug his claws in deeply at every change in position, and the sweet, rich, sharp smell of onion rose around him. Pretty soon he decided that, whatever lay ahead, he would be better able to meet it on a full stomach, so he scraped away the thin outer skin of an onion and began to take bites out of the smooth, soft whiteness. It was juicy and sweet, delicious.

"What are you doing?" asked the voice. "I don't hear you moving, are you all right?"

Fredle swallowed. "Eating," he called back.

"Don't bother. There's always plenty to eat and we were in the middle of a game of Cat. Which you've interrupted."

"Oh," said Fredle. "Sorry." The humor of his apology struck him. "Woo-Hah."

"And stop with the weird noises. You're scaring the mouselets," said the voice.

Fredle could hear how close he was to the other mouse now, and how close to being free. He tasted a change in the air. The air he was breathing now tasted a little damp, not like outside, more like the air behind the refrigerator or the air around the back of the stove. He squeezed forward and found his nose at an opening. After the oniony darkness, the dim light ahead seemed almost bright. He stuck his head and shoulders through the opening and saw, standing right before him, a fat gray mouse.

"Come on out and introduce yourself. All clear, mouselets," the mouse called, turning away from Fredle. "It's a house mouse, just like us."

Fredle hesitated.

"Not far now," the mouse said. "This is the last leg. Are you up to it?" he asked Fredle. Then he called down again, "Back to your nests, all of you. That's all the games for tonight. Tell your mothers we've got company."

There was a muffled chattering and scurrying from below. Fredle didn't move.

The mouse said, "This is a wooden shelf. You can see I'm standing on it. It's perfectly safe."

So Fredle crawled all the way out.

This mouse, despite his size, didn't look strong. He looked

well fed, not fierce. He sat back on his round haunches, giving Fredle time to have a good stare and having a good stare right back at Fredle.

What that mouse *didn't* look was at all nervous. How could a mouse out on a shelf not be nervous?

"I'm Tarnu," said the mouse, and cocked his ears forward.

"Fredle."

"You need to catch your breath? Rest up? Crawl back in for a little more food?" Tarnu asked. "We've got time. Or would you rather have some carrot? Potato? Apple? That's what we eat here, onion, potato, carrot, apple. Nothing fancy, but there's always a lot in the baskets."

Fredle tried to see where he was. There was a foundation wall on one side and open space on the other, with, ahead, another round container just like the one he'd just come out of.

"You're a cellar mouse," he said.

"Got it in one, friend. What about yourself?"

"Kitchen."

"You're used to a wider variety of eats, I bet. But what were you doing in our onion basket? No, don't answer that yet. Everyone will want to hear. Have you decided that you're going to trust me?" Tarnu asked.

"Yes," Fredle said, and he had. He was also quite curious about how this mouse got so relaxed and calm, even when a stranger showed up in the middle of his private food supply.

"It's not hard to get down to the floor from here," Tarnu said to his uninvited guest. "Keep close. If you fall behind, I'll wait."

"What about predators?" asked Fredle.

"What kind of predator would there be in the cellar?"

"There's the cat. Patches."

"Nope."

"There are traps."

"Not here. They don't have any idea we're living down here. Either that or we don't bother them, so they don't bother with us. You almost never see Mister in the cellar, and Missus only comes to use her machines and that's only in daytime. She's no trouble. Shall we go?" And he turned and moved away.

Fredle followed, even more curious. *No predators?* He couldn't imagine it.

They crossed in front of two more baskets and that was the end of the board. Tarnu waited for Fredle to catch up with him before explaining, "This wall is easy to climb up, or down. They used such big stones, see? There's no trick to it. You can follow me or go your own way, whatever." He stepped off onto a big stone that stuck out of the mortar like one of the steps, outside.

Fredle continued to follow Tarnu. Soon he stood on a cool, pleasantly moist dirt floor. Large, curved shapes stood in the distant shadows, motionless, and small things scurried along the floor close by.

"You're in trouble with me now, mouselets," Tarnu said, but he didn't sound angry, or even impatient.

"Big trouble," said the little voices, "big, big trouble," and *they* didn't sound frightened or even worried. "Who's that, Tarnu?"

"It's Fredle. He's a kitchen mouse."

"Did he escape to come live with us?"

"I thought kitchen mice were only in stories."

"He's not so big."

"But he looks tough. Don't you think?"

"I think he looks normal."

"But skinny."

"Yeah, skinny."

"How'd he get here?"

"Yeah, how'd he get here, Tarnu?"

"Give him a minute and he'll tell us. You *will* tell us, won't you, Fredle? So, since I'm guessing that you mouselets aren't about to go back to your nests, I'm going to give you a job. Go get everyone together. We'll be waiting in front of the water heater. Call everyone."

After the mouselets ran off, Tarnu said to Fredle, "I hope it's an exciting story. We like an exciting story, and a long one, too. But I lied to you. I didn't mean to, but I lied about predators. Sometimes—see up there?" He pointed with his nose to the wall far across from them, in front of which stood two square white shapes.

Fredle looked and saw the shapes, with pipes rising up behind one, and above them a window in the wall. Through the window, he could see air that shone a little brighter than the dark air of the cellar.

"I don't know what that's called, or what it's for—" Tarnu began.

"It's a window. You can see through it," Fredle said helpfully.

"Really? Who'd have thought. But why would they want something like that in their walls?"

"To look outside."

"What's to see outside?" Fredle took a breath to tell him, but Tarnu was already going on. "About predators. There's a time, usually the same time as the carrots and onions and potatoes are running out—the apples always run out first—although we never have to worry, because food hasn't ever run entirely out . . . Anyway, during that time, Missus sometimes moves that thing, that window, and the air that comes in is warmer, and smells fresher."

Fredle interrupted. "Summertime, I bet."

"Whatever. And it's not that there's anything wrong with our air, it's just something she likes to do, and when she does that, sometimes, there are a couple of cats that come in through it."

"The barn cats," Fredle guessed. "One's white and the other's black-and-white?"

"Is there anything you don't know?" Tarnu asked, and Fredle assured him, "Lots. Lots and lots."

"They take one or two of us away, every time, but it doesn't happen often and usually the mice that went are too old or sick to escape with the rest of us. We don't really count those cats as predators at all. It's not as if they come foraging every night. Most of the time that—window, you said?—I like knowing the names of things, it always impresses the mouselets . . . Well, she keeps it this way most of the time, and no cat can come through. So let's get ourselves over to the water heater. It's where we go when we all want to get together, which I should tell you is at least twice a day, often more. You'll stay in my nest, won't you?"

Fredle was too surprised at the invitation to answer, but Tarnu assumed it was accepted and went on. "Ellnu would like that, and we've got space. We're one of the nests behind the oil tank. None of the humans ever go behind the oil tank."

By the time Fredle had been introduced all around and told his story, he was tired out. The cellar mice, gathered in the warmth of the tall water heater, had question after question, but after answering only a few, Fredle had to tell them that he couldn't talk any more, not right then, he was too tired, too—

"Of course, we should have thought," said Tarnu. "It's getting late anyway, almost day. He's sleeping in with us, you'll see him tonight. Come along with me, Fredle."

No mouse scurried close along the wall, no mouse took shelter behind any of the big objects, no mouse listened fearfully for the kind of silence a stalking cat creates. The mice just went off in several directions, across the open dirt floor, chattering away without even lowering their voices. Fredle accompanied Tarnu and his family to a wide, soft, cloth-and-paper nest behind a huge, curved oil tank that stood on four short legs in a back cellar corner. Tarnu told Fredle its name, although he couldn't say what it was used for. There was an unpleasant odor, sharp and bitter and heavy, which had soaked into the dirt beneath the tank, but even that couldn't keep Fredle awake. As soon as he had climbed over the edge of the nest, he was already falling asleep, and the last thing he remembered was wishing he could remember the names of all the mice he'd met. *Gannu . . . Olnu . . . Ladnu . . .*

* * *

That evening, Fredle opened his eyes to see an empty nest. Voices came from beyond the tank, so he went out to find Tarnu and the others, and maybe even something to drink and after that something to eat.

He was greeted by many voices.

"He's awake!"

"It's about time."

"Fredle, I brought you some carrot—do you like carrot?"

"Fredle? Watch me!"

"Aren't you thirsty?"

"You must have been really, really tired."

"Are you going to live with Tarnu and Ellnu in their nest?"

"Do you like onion? I brought you some onion."

"Play with us, Fredle. What games do you know?"

Then everyone grew quiet as the entire group waited for his response. All the round, dark mouse eyes were fixed on him.

"Actually," Fredle told them, "I'm pretty thirsty."

"Come with me, then." Tarnu stepped forward. "I'll bring him straight back," he promised, and led Fredle off across the broad dirt floor to two large white metal boxes. "That's the washer, that's the dryer. It's the washer that has water. On that pipe."

Fredle remembered pipes. They were under the kitchen sink, in the cupboard. He knew how to lick the drops of water off of pipes, so he climbed up the wall to where he could reach the pipe while Tarnu waited patiently below. Drinking, Fredle noticed that some pipes led up, along the stone wall and then across the ceiling above him, which he now saw was made of boards and had long, thin black lines crossing it, as well as the round metal pipes. "What are those?" he asked. "Not the pipes, the black lines. Where do the pipes go, does anyone know? I'm looking for a way to go up," he explained.

"Why would you want to do that?"

"To get back to the kitchen."

"Why would you want to do that?" They had started back to where the others waited. "I'm afraid I don't know anything about those pipes, or the black lines. We don't go up to the ceiling," Tarnu told him. "Our territory is down here, and besides, why would anyone want to leave a place where there is always food and water, and shelter, and almost never any predators?"

As soon as they were back by the water heater, Fredle was barraged with questions that gave him no time to think about anything other than what the mice wanted to know. The questions came in no order. There were just a lot of voices, asking him about outside, and what compost was, how a lattice could protect a nest. They didn't believe him about raptors, he could tell, and he didn't try to convince them. They had heard of snakes, but not raccoons. They wondered why the cat that he said lived in the kitchen was to be seen outside—

"His name is Patches," Fredle told them.

"Cats have names? What do they need with names?"

"Everything has a name," Fredle announced, adding, so as not to sound so bossy, "in my experience."

Was the kitchen cat also a predator? they asked. Was it crowded on their wooden board behind the pantry wall? How did you ever relax, out in the wild, never knowing if you were going to be hot or cold, or even wet? "It's always dry, here," they explained. "It's always this same temperature. That's another reason the cellar's the best place for a mouse."

"Not *always* dry. Sometimes water leaks in through the walls and there are puddles."

"Well, almost always."

They couldn't imagine birds flying through the air. They couldn't imagine the sky or clouds or rain, compost or flowers or birds.

"Are birds like flies? We've seen flies. Only big, really big? Birds that big would be loud as Missus's machines."

"You have to let Fredle play with *us* now. We've waited for a long time," the mouselets told their parents.

So Fredle played Follow-the-Leader (Fredle), after which there was a game of Hide-and-Seek (Fredle was It), then Tickle-and-Run-Fast, and finally Three Blind Mice (Fredle, Ellnu, and a high-spirited young mouse named Linu, who was particularly clever about nosing out the mouselets even with her eyes tightly closed). There was much squealing and laughing and excitement, all night long.

Afterward, when the mouselets were tired out, the families sat around in groups, talking. They reviewed what Fredle had told them, and decided, "It's a terrible place, outside."

"Actually," Fredle said, "it isn't, it's—"

"Makes you appreciate your own home, doesn't it?"

Then they talked much more about the question of whether carrots were sweeter than apples, and about the difference in taste between a new young potato and an older, riper one, and tried to describe to Fredle how to combine different foods in his mouth—apples and onions, potatoes and onions—the possibilities were endless, they said. If you chewed slowly, tasting with full attention, you would find that each food had a new, and wonderful, flavor.

It was a long, lazy night out on the cellar floor. The different families mingled in groups that occasionally changed, the young sometimes staying close to their parents or grandparents, sometimes going off to be with others their own age. If you were thirsty, you went over to the big machine to drink from the pipes. If you were hungry, you made the quick trip up to the baskets and chose what you wanted to eat. Eventually, the dark air grew lighter and the mice began to yawn and go their separate ways to their own nests, for a good day's sleep. For the second time, Fredle went with Tarnu and Ellnu and their mouselets to the nest behind the big, ill-smelling oil tank.

Tarnu apologized. "There *are* some bad smells down here. Over by the machines it's soap, which I personally think is much worse. Oil isn't so bad, once you get used to it."

Fredle could think of no reason to try to convince Tarnu that the fresh air outside was preferable, or the warm, food-flavored kitchen air. He had never seen mice like this, unworried, unafraid, contented. These mice were happy, he realized. They lived every night of their lives in this lazy, easy way and they played with their mouselets on the dirt floor of the cellar as if there were no danger at all. They seemed to understand something about how to be a mouse alive in the world that no other mouse—no other creature—Fredle had ever met had figured out.

Of course, it you didn't have to worry about food, it might be easy to be happy, especially if you almost never had to worry about cats, and never about traps, raptors, or raccoons, either. Whatever the reason, it seemed to Fredle that these cellar mice knew how to enjoy just being awake, eating and talking and playing with their mouselets.

17
The Way Up

Fredle spent several nights in the cellar, answering questions about outside (Colors? Squirrels? Ramps? Stone walls? Trees!) and asking questions of his own (Baskets of food that never ran out? How many different games? How many kinds of spiders?). There was talking, and more talking, about the danger of chocolate and why Missus saved Fredle's life, about ice cream and where outside turned into wild, about why humans liked cats but not mice, and whether another creature, like a dog, like Sadie, could be trusted. Anything that could be thought about or asked about got talked over, in the cellar. Even though he was always thinking about a way back to the upstairs, Fredle enjoyed those nights. He was always sorry when another night had slipped peacefully by and it came time to go to sleep. He was always pleased to wake up and begin another long, easy night. Until, one day, things changed.

They were all asleep in their nests after a busy night of good food, play, and conversation when, suddenly, the weak light from the high windows disappeared in a blast of silent and immediate brightness.

Fredle's eyes snapped open. His heart raced. He looked across at Tarnu and Ellnu, who were sleeping peacefully. In fact, the whole family slept peacefully on, undisturbed. Fredle crawled out of the nest and saw Linu looking out over the rim of her own family's nest, also behind the oil tank. Fredle whispered, "What is it?"

The light was not as bright as sunlight and didn't infuse the air the way sunlight did, but it was uncomfortably bright, especially after the usual dimness of the cellar. Linu said, "There's nothing to worry about. It's just Missus. You want to see her use the machines?"

Of course Fredle did and of course Linu was happy to show him. "It's the only thing that happens here in the cellar, almost. Not like outside, with all your adventures. Not like the kitchen, with its traps and that cat you told us about, with Mister and Missus and the dogs."

"There's a baby, too," Fredle said. He knew he was showing off but he said it anyway.

"Not like the wild, either."

Fredle agreed. In fact, the cellar was just about the absolute opposite of wild.

"The only dangerous thing that happens here is when those two cats come in. Missus isn't at all dangerous. She comes here a lot, sometimes to check the food in our baskets, sometimes like now for the machines. Look."

They had come to the front leg of the oil tank and Fredle saw Missus, at the other end of the cellar, with a tall white container beside her. She was bending down and taking things out of the container to put them into one of the big square machines, which shone whiter than usual in the brightness that now filled the cellar.

A faint, sharp, unpleasant smell—definitely *not* food—floated briefly by his nose, and then it was gone. The machine started making noises and Missus went up some stairs. The light disappeared.

"She'll come back, turn on the other machine, come back again and fill the basket back up, and take it away with her," Linu explained. "Each time, there's light, and then it's gone. But that's not very exciting, is it? Especially not for you."

Fredle couldn't argue about that. Instead, he said, "I'm looking for a way to get upstairs."

"I know. We're all trying to think of one. Could you sneak into Missus's container?"

"That's too dangerous. Is that the only idea you've had?"

"Why don't you want to go back outside?"

"Upstairs is home. Besides, I already know how to get back outside, if I want to."

"Are there flowers upstairs? I think I'd rather see flowers than stars. Which do you like better, Fredle?"

"Woo-Hah," Fredle laughed. "Both."

"Maybe I do, too," Linu said. Then she said, looking around at the cellar with its shelves of food and unseen families of sleeping mice, "I'm sorry I don't know a way for you to get home, Fredle. Do you want to look for one together? We could look tonight."

"Why not now?"

"Now? It's daytime. Mice sleep during the day."

"We're not asleep," Fredle pointed out. "Anyway, since I'm awake I'm going to do it. Come on along if you want to." He actually hoped she would want to join him in the search, because things were more enjoyable when you had company. But he would go looking, with or without her.

"All right," Linu said. "I've been thinking about upstairs. It's pretty easy to see that to get there you'd have to find a way through the ceiling. So," she finished, in case Fredle couldn't think it out for himself, "the first thing is, you have to find a way to the ceiling."

They both looked up.

The ceiling was not made of impenetrable stones and mortar, like the cellar walls. It was made out of strips of wood, like the cupboard shelves. Wooden boards ran across it, and there were also the round white pipes, as well as the long black lines. Linu was right; Fredle knew that as soon as she had spoken. The ceiling was the only possible entrance to upstairs.

Was it possible to move across the ceiling? Upside down? He couldn't imagine it. But that was a problem he couldn't solve from down below. If it *was* possible, he wouldn't see how until he actually got up there.

The first thing, then, was to find a way up the wall. Fredle and Linu climbed to the shelves where the baskets stood, which was a known and easy path, and from there, continuing slowly, they found footholds on stones that jutted out from the wall. When they had arrived at the top of the wall, they discovered a board just wide enough to walk along single file. That was easier going, and for mice, with their natural balance and light-footedness, not perilous.

However, they had no known route to follow. They were exploring.

Fredle looked all around, noticing everything he could, and he thought. He wondered aloud, "Where do the pipes go?" and he answered himself, "Upstairs. I've seen pipes in the kitchen. In the sink cupboard."

"They look like they go through holes in the ceiling, don't you think? See?" Linu asked. "Can you see a board that leads over to the pipes? I think this one—" And she was off.

"Don't go too fast," Fredle advised, and followed her.

They were in the middle of the ceiling when once again light exploded all around them. This time, Fredle knew enough to simply freeze where he was. He looked down at Missus from above, and she didn't look so very big after all, bending to take things out of one machine and put them into the other, which immediately started making its own rumbling noises, like hundreds of raccoons, snoring. Then she went out of sight. When they could no longer hear her footsteps ascending, the light disappeared again. After a while, "Is it safe now?" Fredle asked.

"Did you see how high we are? I didn't know you could get up onto these boards and be so high. You *are* an adventurer, Fredle."

Fredle was surprised to hear that, but he didn't mind. "Maybe I am, sometimes," he said.

"I think we can get from here to the pipes that go from the

top of the water heater," she told him. "We can get to a lot of new places from here."

Moving quickly but carefully, because you wouldn't want to fall from so high up, they made their way across to the boards that crossed above the water heater. Standing there, looking up, they could see a pipe entering the ceiling through a hole large enough for a mouse to squeeze through.

"What did I say?" asked Linu.

"And you were right!"

For a while, they looked at it. Then they talked about how easy it would be for a mouse to get up there from where they stood, and Fredle knew that he was almost home. He turned to Linu.

"Make my farewells to everyone. Especially Tarnu. Can you remember that?"

"I'm not silly," she told him crossly. "Of course I can. But, Fredle?"

"What's wrong? Do you want to come, too?" Fredle hadn't thought of that before, but now that he had he wondered what Linu would think of life in the kitchen, and wondered how the kitchen mice would react to learning what it was really like to live in the cellar. Now that he had thought of it, he rather hoped she would come with him.

But she was shaking her head. "I better not."

"If you know the way to get there, then you also know the way back," he told her.

Linu continued shaking her head, but she said, "I'd have to say goodbye, and explain where I'd be, and tell them I'd be with you so I'd be safe."

Then Fredle was shaking *his* head. He had learned that if you didn't get going right away—if, for example, you went back to say goodbye or take a last look at the stars—then something might easily happen to keep you from ever reaching your destination. Or even to make you went. If reaching your destination was important, you couldn't hesitate. "I can't wait," he apologized to Linu.

Just as he was saying that, she was saying, a little sadly, "I can't go."

So they parted, Linu to retrace her steps along the boards and Fredle to go along the pipe until it turned up, into the ceiling, into the house above.

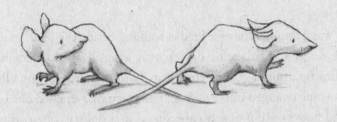

18
The Return

It was a long journey for Fredle, walking beside the pipe where he could and balancing on top of it when he had to, scrambling up insulation and across thin, narrow boards. Eventually, the pipe emerged into a dark, closed place that smelled of soap and flowers. Rolls of soft paper stood in a stack in one corner. There was nothing at all familiar about the place, although it did smell faintly of mouse, as if once, long ago, a family of mice had lived there. What kind of mice would they have been? Fredle wondered. But they weren't there now and he didn't want to linger. The darkness was too thick; it lay too heavy on his eyes and skin. He knew he had arrived upstairs, but this wasn't the part of upstairs he was looking for, so he went back down the pipe, back inside the walls and along to where the pipe next went up, to enter another enclosed space.

This space was not as dark as the first. It had doors, one of which was not fully closed. Moreover, the soapy smells here were sharp and familiar, and so were the boxes and soft sponges and stiff brushes and folded pieces of cloth through which Fredle clambered, moving hastily in his excitement, heading for the light. He knew where he was. When he went cautiously up to the opened door and looked out, he saw the kitchen.

It was light in the kitchen, although not as bright as daytime outside. From his hiding place, Fredle couldn't see any movement, but he heard human voices, and the baby fussing. He heard the soft click of dog nails on the floor. He waited, listening, trying to understand what he was seeing, to identify something he had previously seen only in darkness.

He smelled food. He could now identify one of the smells as chicken, but that was the only familiar odor.

He heard Mister say, "This is the best chicken noodle soup you've ever made, honey."

"You always say that," Missus answered.

"It's always true," Mister said.

"And I always tell you, the secret is lots of bones in the stock. But *do* you think the baby is running a temperature?"

"She's teething, that's all."

"Should I call the doctor?" asked Missus.

"If it'll make you feel better," said Mister. "Angus and I are taking the truck up to check on the sheep and then I'll be in the cornfield until supper. That's where I'll be if you need me."

All of this time, the baby was fussing away, not crying, just making little unhappy, dissatisfied sounds.

"You know where *I'll* be," Missus answered.

There was a scraping sound, and "Angus? Come," Mister said. Fredle watched shadows moving across the black-and-white floor.

A voice quite close to him said, "Fredle? What are you doing in there?"

Fredle froze.

"I know it's you. Didn't you hear me?"

Before he could answer, Missus had called Sadie away. "That stuff under the sink will make you sick, you know that, you silly girl." Then the door shut tight, leaving Fredle once again in darkness.

Then he could only hear the muffled sounds of the baby and a rushing sound in the pipes, as if a stream were running through them.

He waited.

The watery sound ceased and then he could no longer hear the baby. It would still be day, out there in the kitchen, he thought. He knew he should wait where he was, in safety, until night. But he had waited so long, he had been waiting since the long-ago day Missus carried him outside, and he could wait no longer.

The cupboard door was now firmly closed, so Fredle returned to the wall. This was a path he knew, following the pipes under the sink to get inside the wall behind the stove and from there over to the pantry. From the pipes, Fredle could travel within the closeness of the walls without any fear of predators—safe, inside, making the long, slow journey home. Or he could enter the kitchen through the hole behind the stove, from which it was only a short dash across to the pantry door and the quickest way home.

When he came out behind the stove, Fredle turned *that* way, and when he came to the end of the narrow passage between stove and wall, he stuck a wary nose out to be sure the kitchen was empty.

With a soft thud, the cat landed just in front of him.

Fredle didn't even stop to think. He ran. Ran back into the passage, out of reach of that long, clawed leg. *Then* he froze.

"Well, well," Patches purred. "It's Sadie's little friend."

Fredle was relieved to hear that. "Yes," he said. "Fredle."

The cat's paw groped into the narrow space, long nails scraping on the wall and floor. Fredle protested, "I'm Sadie's friend, remember?"

"That will be useful to you the next time we meet outside," Patches said. He didn't sound at all unfriendly. "But at present you are *inside*. Although you do seem to have caught that bad outside habit of running away."

Fredle didn't bother answering. He was considering his situation. Cats, he knew, were patient. Mice, on the other hand, are by nature panicky. But Fredle had more sense than to run straight into a cat's claws just because that was the straightest way home. He knew there was the other route. He would rather have entered the pantry through the hole at the bottom of the door and gone from there into the walls for a quick climb home, but that was no longer a choice.

Patches settled his body down into the crouch position, his tail waving back and forth along the floor.

Fredle squeezed himself around to go back into the wall and begin the difficult ascending pathway along beams and insulation.

There was the usual lightlessness within the walls, but he had so often followed Axle up and down this path that his feet remembered the way, and he still remembered exactly where it was necessary to go very carefully and where he could move without paying such close attention.

Taking this path reminded him of Axle, and he hoped she had made it safely to the attic. He already knew, although he hadn't realized it until just then, that she hadn't gone to the cellar. If she had, the cellar mice would have welcomed her, and fed her, and made her one of them, unless she had chosen, as he had, to return home. But even in that case, the cellar mice would still be talking about her. Axle would have been— just as Fredle was sure he himself was now—one of their best stories, to tell and retell in the gatherings by the water heater.

Fredle climbed and wondered and wished Axle well, wherever she had ended up. As long as she didn't went, he could be happy for her.

Arriving at last at the wide familiar board, Fredle stopped, to breathe everything in, the dimness, the sound of snoring and rustling and an occasional cough or whimper, the dusty, mousey smell of the air and the sight of two pale nests lying between tall wood-and-plaster walls. Then all of his attention turned to that corner nest, the one he was at last approaching, coming up to the side of, crawling over the edge of.

Home was warm with the bodies of sleeping mice. As if he were only coming back late from a foraging expedition and his arrival was not worth waking up for, the various bodies shifted around to allow him to take his usual place next to Kidle, where he fell immediately into a deep, restful sleep.

19
Home

Fredle opened his eyes to see Kidle staring down at him in happy surprise.

"Where'd you come from? Father! It's Fredle! Mother? Grandfather? It's Fredle! He's come back!"

Fredle stood up, feeling a little foolish and very proud. They were all looking at him, absolutely amazed, all the remembered faces plus several new and unknown ones.

"There's no need to shriek, Kidle," said Father, and then Mother said, "It can't be," and Father asked cautiously, "Fredle?" as if unable to believe his own eyes and nose.

"I thought I'd never see you again," Grandfather said.

They crowded close around him, touching him with their cool, pointed noses.

"Woo-Hah," Fredle laughed, out of sheer happiness.

"What did he say?" Mother asked Father.

"That didn't sound like our Fredle," said Father.

"What if it's not? What if it's a danger to the mouselets?"

"It is me, Mother," said Fredle. "It really is."

"You look different," she complained.

"No he doesn't," Kidle disagreed.

"Grown-up," Grandfather diagnosed. "Like Axle."

Axle? It seemed that Fredle's perfect happiness could grow more perfect. Was that possible? "Axle?" he asked.

"She came back a couple of nights after—" Father stopped. Then he said, "All right, everyone. Everyone awake? It's time."

"Doddle isn't ready," said Mother. "He's just a mouselet and I don't like to leave him alone. It's just sleepiness, I'm sure he's not sick, but—"

"If a mouselet can't forage, we have to push him out," said Father.

"Besides," said Landle, one of Fredle's many brothers, "you've been saying there are already too many of us. And now there's Fredle, too."

"I could bring back something for Doddle," Fredle offered. "For him and for you, Mother."

"Mice don't do that," Father said.

"I know, but why don't we?" Fredle asked.

"You haven't been back one night and already you're starting with the questions," said Father.

Grandfather was more patient. "You know we don't eat in our nests, young Fredle. Besides, you don't want to begin carrying food around for other mice. Trust me, I know. That kind of thing leads to nothing but trouble."

"How?" asked Fredle. If Grandfather knew something dangerous that happened as a result of helping out another mouse, Fredle thought he wanted to know what that was. "How do you know?"

"It's Fredle for sure," said Father gloomily. "All right, everybody. We can talk later, but right now we have foraging to do. Everybody in place if you plan to eat tonight."

Fredle wanted to ask about Axle, but now he was remembering how the evenings were always arranged. Forage first, and then, after, if there was the chance, you could talk. He wondered if he really could hope that Axle, too, had been able to escape the worst consequences of eating chocolate. He wondered if she knew it was called chocolate. He thought she would be impressed by everything that had happened to him and would want to hear all about all of it. She used to be the one telling her adventures and now he had adventures of his own to tell her.

Following Father's quiet progress down to the pantry floor entryway, he got close enough to Grandfather to whisper, "Is Axle really and truly alive?"

"Of course. She's young and strong. I'm the one you should be surprised to find still here."

That was good enough for Fredle, for the time being. He could wait to hear the details. He was content to be back in his usual place between Grandfather and Kidle, one of a line of mice creeping out into the kitchen to forage. Being home, with familiar mice all around him, familiar boards under his feet and the familiar dim light all around, knowing where he would look for food and what he might find, knowing that somewhere ahead in the night kitchen Axle was foraging (and wouldn't she be surprised to see him!), Fredle had the feeling that nothing had changed.

It was a wonderful, comfortable feeling. It was the feeling he had been longing for ever since he had been shoved down along the wall and pushed out onto the pantry floor. He was home, where Father and Grandfather knew what a mouse had to do, where they had their own nightly routines, where he knew what the dangers were, and where Father's family had its own territory, its very own section of the board behind the pantry wall, trespassed upon only by the occasional ant or spider. Within the walls, a mouse could move in perfect safety from the kitchen to his nest, or to the cupboard under the sink and the narrow space behind the stove. Fredle felt once again that he was a very lucky mouse. He had had an adventure and he had come safely home.

He found Axle foraging under the table. "Axle!" he cried.

"You?" she gasped. "I never thought— I thought— Fredle? Is that you, really?"

"Woo-Hah," he laughed. "Yes, it is."

"Quiet!" she warned him.

Fredle lowered his voice. "Am I glad to see *you*. How did you—"

"You know the rule, Fredle. *Forage comes first.* I'll try to come to your nest, later, after. Talking now is too risky."

Axle was as bossy as ever, but Fredle didn't mind. He was so glad to see her strong, gray body and round, dark eyes, and the familiar curve of her half-ear that—now that he had seen them, he knew—resembled one of the moons he had glimpsed in the night sky.

He couldn't wait to tell Axle about the moons and the stars, the compost and the raccoons—especially the raccoons. Axle would enjoy those raccoons. He would be able to admit to her that it was his sweet tooth that got him into that particular bit of trouble, too. She'd like that, and she'd understand the temptation.

Fredle's foraging didn't go particularly well. He found only one kibbles; it was enough to fill his stomach, but its dry tastelessness only made him think about the sweetness of onions and apples, the crisp freshness of ramps and bitter chewiness of orange peel, all the good things he'd learned to eat. After a trip into the kitchen sink cupboard for water, he was ready to return to the nest.

The others, however, weren't. "Don't *rush* us," Father said crossly. "The mouselets aren't experienced foragers like you, Fredle. I don't know *what* kind of bad habits you've picked up wherever you've been, but you can start getting rid of them right now."

Father grumbled on. "*And* two of those mouselets can never find themselves enough to eat. Of course they're failing to flourish, what does your mother expect to happen? What does she think I can do about it?"

"Um-hmm," answered Fredle. This was a downside to having been away for so long: you had to catch up on all the bad things that had happened while you weren't there.

Or maybe, he thought, it was a downside to coming back?

And then he wondered: Was Father sorry that he had come back?

The foraging continued and Fredle waited by the pantry door, alert for Patches. He heard Mother's voice telling the mouselets, "Hurry up, it's dangerous. You can't *still* be hungry, Ardle. Stay close, Doddle. Remember the cat, everyone—Idle, *NO!*"

He heard other whispered comments: "Hungry season coming, mark my words." "Used to be, there were more crumbs under the table." "Was that the cat?" "Used to be, there were always kibbles."

Grandfather came to stand near Fredle, within easy reach of the hole through the pantry door. "You've come back to hard times, young Fredle."

"You know, Grandfather? Down in the cellar there's—" Fredle began, but he was interrupted.

"I'm glad I'll soon be went. It won't be too long now."

Fredle wanted to deny this, but it was true. Grandfather *was* old. Hoping to cheer the old mouse up, he started to tell Grandfather what had happened to him, even though Grandfather hadn't asked. "I was outside, Missus carried me outside. At night, outside, it's dark, not dim like inside. Outside, it's a bright darkness and sometimes there's a moon. Grandfather? Or maybe it's a lot of moons, I don't know, nobody knows, but a moon is like . . ." He tried to think of what a moon *was* like. "Like a white circle that shines out light. It floats in the dark air, way up high, and only at night. It's nocturnal, like mice."

He waited, but Grandfather had nothing to say to this. Grandfather just stared into the shadowy kitchen and waited.

"And in daylight—which is so bright, you can't imagine it—there are colors," Fredle went on. But Grandfather hadn't even looked at him, so he stopped trying to talk and turned his attention back to listening. He listened to Mother's worried voice urging the mouselets to hurry up, and Father saying, "Stop that chattering, you two, just stop it."

Then, after a long time, Grandfather did speak, so softly it was almost a whisper. "Moon. What a word that is. There's a word to dream about, *moon*. Hear it, Fredle?"

Father came up to the door in time to hear this. "Get started, Grandfather. You know you're slow and we can't always be waiting for you."

Fredle heard a dog bark, too far off for him to know if it was Angus or Sadie, and he wondered if the dog was barking at something seen through a window, out in the garden or near the chicken pen, or moving across in front of the barn. He heard faint baby cries, and then Father had gathered his whole family together, to file back up to the nest.

There Fredle curled up beside Kidle. "Are you still hungry?" Kidle asked. "I am."

"You want to go back down and forage some more?" Fredle offered.

"We can't do that. It's almost day, and besides, what if Father found out?"

"But—" Fredle began, but Kidle said, "It'll be all right once I go to sleep. Maybe tomorrow night will be better, don't you think?"

Soon, Fredle's whole family was asleep. Fredle rested his head on the rim of the nest to make it easy for Axle to find him. He waited and waited, but Axle did not come. Eventually, he fell asleep himself.

Fredle didn't sleep deeply, however, and he didn't sleep well. He woke up several times during the day and had to wait patiently, motionless so as not to disturb the others, for sleep to return.

* * *

The next night, after foraging briefly and with enough success to keep his stomach quiet through the next day, he set out to find Axle. He looked under the table and around the refrigerator, and finally found her beside the stove. "You didn't—" he started to say.

"I forgot," she said, so quickly that he knew he couldn't believe her. "You didn't come find me, either."

"I thought you said—"

Axle shook her head. She didn't want to hear this. She looked right at Fredle. "I don't know what happened to you, all this time you've been gone, but it must have been better than what happened to me. A lot better."

Fredle had been looking forward to telling Axle his story. "Well, it was Missus who—"

"I was trying to find a way up to the attic, where they're not cellar mice, dirty, and half-crazy from eating soap. I thought I could stand it, up with the attic mice, I could learn to eat the weird things they eat, cloth and wood and insulation. But I couldn't find the way and I was all alone in some spidery corner between the kitchen and the attic, somewhere, I didn't know where, and I was so thirsty. I just barely had the strength to creep into a cupboard—not the kitchen one, but I could smell water, and there were pipes, like in the kitchen, and paper, in rolls, in a stack. I ate soap, Fredle."

"I think I was there, too!" Fredle cried. "I smelled—"

"I was in that cupboard for nights! Where else could I go? It was so dark," Axle remembered. "I had to eat that paper. I was alone. I was all alone, Fredle."

"I know about that," Fredle said. "When I was alone—"

"I couldn't sleep, there was only that paper to eat, except for soap, it was . . . I *hated* it. I was alone," she said again, as if that explained everything. "So I came back."

She glared at Fredle.

"It took me a long time to find the way home," he told her, so that she would know that he, too, had wanted to come back.

"They let me stay. I was sure they'd push me out, even though by then I was fine again, but they never even mentioned it. We never figured it out, Fredle. We just didn't understand. We treated it like some game, but—it's— Bad things happen when you break the rules."

"I know," Fredle said, first remembering how glad he'd been to see Bardo and then almost wishing he could see Neldo and her brother again. "But not always, not all bad."

Axle continued. "Something was bound to happen, sooner or later. We were heading for trouble. I *was* sorry to hear you got pushed out."

Fredle waited for her to ask him about what had happened to him, how he had managed, where he had gone and what he had seen, but she didn't have a single question. Instead, she told him, "It's getting pretty crowded behind the pantry."

"In the cellar—"

"A lot of the mouselets will have to be pushed out, unless we all want to go hungry. It's not easy, these days," Axle said. Then she *did* have a question. "Where are you going?"

Fredle had turned around to leave. He looked back to explain, "I want to . . ." But he was too sad to say more.

He went to wait by the pantry door with Grandfather. Grandfather didn't even greet him, he just said, "Really and truly? Up in the air? Moons?"

Fredle was glad to be able to say to him, "Really and truly."

"I wish I wasn't old," Grandfather said.

"You'd like the lattice wall, too," Fredle said, wishing the same thing. "You can see through it, to outside and the green of the grass, and—"

"I don't know," Grandfather answered quietly, but he didn't tell Fredle if what he didn't know had to do with grass and the lattice wall or with something else. "I just don't know."

As they made the trip back up to their nest, Fredle asked Kidle, "Is something wrong with Grandfather?"

"He's worried about how we'll manage. I think he expects, any day, that he'll be the one pushed out."

"I shouldn't have come back."

"That's not it," Kidle assured him. "We're all glad and I'm *really* glad. It's only, what Father says, it's hard times."

"What can we do to make them better?" Fredle asked.

"When times are hard, all a mouse can do is hunker down. That's the way mice are."

Not me, Fredle wanted to tell him, but first he wanted to talk to Axle again. That is, he wanted to *try* to talk to Axle. He wanted to give her another chance.

So before he went to sleep, he crept back along the board to her family's nest. "Axle?" he whispered. "Axle!" and eventually he saw her head rise over the rim. "Come down," he said.

"I can't. You know that, Fredle."

"I wanted to tell you," he whispered. "I met raccoons."

"Raccoons?"

"A band of them, they were going to eat me—*after* they showed me the lake and fed me some fish. But I escaped."

"You don't expect me to believe that, do you?" Axle asked. "We're too old for stories now, Fredle," she told him. "I've grown up and you should have, too."

"And there were stars," said Fredle, desperately.

Axle didn't ask him what any of those things might be, stars, or fish, or lake, and she didn't ask him what raccoons looked like and smelled like, or talked about. "Go to sleep, Fredle," she advised him. "That's what I'm going to do. That's all a mouse can do when he has to go to bed hungry."

Fredle didn't move. "In the cellar—" he tried again, but she was gone.

Fredle didn't want to return to his nest. He wasn't tired. But where could he go? Here, inside, within the walls, there was no place to go, and even if you got somewhere, it would be just like the place you left. Everything was the same, here, inside, he thought. Everything didn't change and mice didn't change and the way things were was the way things had to be. He had certainly heard the rules often enough.

Thinking that made Fredle tired, but not in the way that made him simply want to sleep. He was tired in a way that made him not want to *do* anything except go back to the nest and wait for sleep to come and find him. He turned slowly around.

Why couldn't mice change? he wondered tiredly. And

then he was awake and paying full attention to his own question because he knew that he *had* changed. He had changed, and not just once but many times. This thought gave him a surge of energy and he no longer had any desire to return to the nest. Instead, moving along within the walls so as to be safe (he hadn't changed *that* much; it would be really stupid for a mouse not to worry about safety), he made his way to the cabinet under the kitchen sink, hoping that once again the door would be open and maybe he could hear something happening or—this would be the best—maybe he would have a chance to talk with Sadie.

The cupboard door *was* open and there was sunlight in the kitchen, some of which brightened the space under the sink, where Fredle hid himself between a tall green box and a round white container, both stinking of soap. Fredle heard Mister and Missus talking. He didn't hear the dogs.

"I'm worried," Missus said.

"I am, too," Mister answered.

"But I'm *really* worried now. She's sleeping but I gave her Tylenol, so that's why."

"If her temperature goes up again, or goes above a hundred and two, we'll swing into action. What do you say to that? I'll work in the barn today, or maybe in the garden. I'll keep close by."

"I'm way behind on the weeding."

"You're worried, it's understandable; it keeps you busy, having a baby, the baby being sick," Mister said. "Sadie? Angus? Let's go down to the barn and give our ladies some peace and quiet."

For some reason, overhearing this conversation and the sounds of the two dogs getting up, their nails clicking on the floor, their steps following Mister's steps away, and the snap of the door, closing, made Fredle feel better. Less uneasy. He went back up to his nest and fell asleep.

20

In the End

That night, something happened in the kitchen that had never happened before, not in Father's memory or Grandfather's, either. As the mice foraged, scattered into the shadowy corners of the kitchen, light broke out, all around them, a light so bright that for a few seconds nobody could see anything.

Under the table and behind the stove or refrigerator, mice froze, and two unfortunate mice froze where they were in the wide, empty space between the stove and the table, between pantry and refrigerator.

The cat pounced.

Mister stood by the counter and paid no attention to cat or mouse. He started talking to someone, but not Angus, although Angus stood at his side and, at the sound of Mister's low, hurried words, looked up into his face. Then Missus rushed in, carrying the baby, who was fussing unhappily but rather quietly, as if she didn't have the energy to really cry.

"The hospital's expecting us," Mister said. "Let's go, Angus. Sadie? Where *is* that dog?"

"She's gone to ground, I expect. It's what she does when there's trouble, or thunder. Under our bed or in the baby's closet. Should I—"

"She'll be all right. I just thought they'd be better off outside. We don't know how long we'll be."

"No, we don't. Do we."

"It'll be fine, I hope."

"Babies run high temperatures all the time. I do know that."

Then Mister and Missus, the baby, and Angus left the room and the door closed behind them. But the light stayed on.

After many long moments, the mice moved, scurrying to get safely back to their entryways—the pantry door, the hole behind the stove—foraging forgotten in their fear and their hope to be safe. The cat pounced again, and after that there was only silence.

When the light had burst out, Fredle had been at the far end of the kitchen, chasing a pea around one of the table legs. He froze, but not from fear or for safety. It was the sight of colors that stopped him in his tracks. He had already forgotten how many colors there were, when there was light, and he looked around at the brown of the table leg, the black and white of the floor, and an orange chunk of carrot that had rolled up against the wall. He had already swallowed the pea, so he couldn't enjoy its greenness. When the humans and the dog had left the room, he'd chosen not to join the run back to the pantry door. He listened for the cat, and watched for him, and hoped that Grandfather, who was so slow now, had as usual finished his foraging early and been at the pantry door when the lights went on. He hoped that the mouselets had been near Mother, who would have kept them safe. Although, he thought—because mice have to be practical about this—if the cat got them, got Doddle, for example, the nest would have one less mouth to feed.

Just where Patches was, Fredle didn't know, and he wasn't about to move until he did. How long that would be, he couldn't guess. However, before he had located the cat, he heard Sadie clicking into the kitchen and saw her go to her water bowl to drink. "Sadie!" he called, in the loudest whisper he could manage. "Sadie!"

Dogs have fine hearing. Sadie lifted her head and looked around. "Fredle?"

"Over here, under here."

She found him easily. "What are you doing?" she asked, not even lowering her voice. "Inside, I mean, and here, too, now. Why are you under our table? The baby is sick," she told him. "The baby is very sick."

"I saw them carry her out." Fredle could understand why Sadie sounded so sad. Her job was to take care of the baby and now the baby was sick. With the baby gone, she didn't have a job.

"Everyone had loud voices, so I went under the bed. They ran around. When I'm under the bed I'm not in the way," Sadie explained. "But I think I should have come down. Angus came down."

"He went outside through the door," Fredle told her.

"Being under the bed doesn't make the worry stop," Sadie told him.

"I'm sorry, Sadie." Fredle didn't blame her for being upset. He didn't know what the humans would do with a dog who didn't have a job.

"It's nicer to be worried *with* someone."

"What will your new job be?"

She was surprised. "Am I having a new job? Will I be good at it?"

Fredle spoke in a gentle and sympathetic voice, reminding her, "They've taken the baby away."

"Is somebody else going to take care of the baby? Is Patches? Angus has to be trained and win ribbons in shows and herd sheep, so he can't do it. But I do a good job. Missus says."

Fredle was about to explain about went, and being sick and being pushed out, but he heard Patches padding softly toward them and scurried to safety underneath Sadie's stomach.

"Is that that mouse? That Fredle?"

"He's talking to me," Sadie said.

From his safe position, Fredle pointed out, "You've already eaten two mice. You can't be hungry."

"You should go away, Patches. You make Fredle worry."

That was certainly true.

Patches said, "You can't hide him there forever."

"Oh," said Sadie. "He's right, Fredle, I can't. I'm sorry."

Fredle wasn't sure what might happen next if he didn't speak up, so he spoke up. "We could walk together over to the stove, you and me, and when we get there I could get behind it, where Patches can't reach me. Then I could wait with you, and worry with you, too, without being went."

It was a good idea, so it was what they did.

Patches watched this operation, and yawned. "What good does worrying do?" he asked. "What good does worrying do either one of you?"

"I can't help it," Sadie answered.

"Cats know better than to worry," Patches said.

When Fredle had settled himself safely behind the metal mass of stove, Sadie lay down close beside it and Patches went back to wherever cats go. From the narrow space behind the stove Fredle could see Sadie's brown-and-white fur, and he could also see flowers in a glass on the table, tall yellow flowers among their green leaves. He knew he should go back to the nest, but he didn't want to stop seeing colors, not yet. Soon enough he would be back in the dim gray light.

From outside, Angus barked. "Sadie? Sadie, can you hear me? They took the baby."

"I'm in the kitchen!"

"They took the baby in the car."

"I'm waiting inside!" barked Sadie.

Fredle tried to think of something to cheer Sadie up. "Maybe they'll get another baby and you can have the job of taking care of that one."

"But I already have this one. I can't take care of two."

"But they took this one away," Fredle reminded her. Sadie really *was* forgetful.

"But they're going to bring her back. After the vet fixes her."

"The baby's sick, Sadie. Sick things don't come back. They get pushed out to went."

"When my leg was broken, the vet fixed it. That's the vet's job, to make you better, and when that's done you come home."

This sounded unhappily like the moonbits story to Fredle, but Sadie seemed confident of her information. "Then why are you worried?" he asked.

"At night, we all go to sleep until morning," Sadie explained. "But now it's night and Angus is outside and I'm alone inside. You're inside, too," she added in case Fredle had forgotten that, reminding him, "You used to be outside."

"I did," he agreed. He tried one last time to get Sadie ready. "What makes you so sure they won't push the baby out?"

"Why would they do that? That would scare her, and she'd cry. She doesn't like to be alone," Sadie told him.

Fredle gave up. Poor Sadie would find out the truth, soon enough. He just waited with her, the dog stretched out on the floor beside the stove behind which the mouse sat, waiting. Every now and then Sadie sighed, and shifted her nose from one paw to the other. They didn't talk, they just waited.

Fredle did wonder why he cared about what happened to Sadie. Then he remembered that the bravest thing he had ever done had to do with Sadie and her baby. The good feeling that memory gave him made him feel connected to Sadie and made him want to be there to comfort her when Mister and Missus came back home without the baby and she realized that Fredle had been right.

After a long, long time, Angus barked again, even more loudly. "Hello! Hello!"

Sadie jumped up and ran to the door, also barking, "Hello! I'm in the kitchen! I came downstairs, I'm sorry!"

Fredle crept as close as he dared to the stove's edge.

Heavy footsteps sounded from outside and the door opened. Fredle didn't dare stick his head out to see. He couldn't be sure where Patches was and he knew that without Sadie next to him, he wasn't safe from Patches, inside. So he listened as hard as he could, to find out.

"You should have obeyed. Mister called you and you didn't obey. They wanted us to be outside and they were already worried. You have to obey better, Sadie."

"I know. I was sorry right away. But Fredle was here."

"Fredle? Never mind that, I'm telling you something important."

"Good boy, Angus," Mister said. "Hello, Sadie, you're a good dog, too. You OK, honey?"

"Fine," Missus said, in a tired voice.

Poor Sadie, Fredle thought. Nobody was saying anything about any baby and he knew what that meant. Angus wasn't being very sympathetic, either.

Missus said, "Turn off the lights, will you? We don't want to wake the baby." Suddenly the light disappeared and the colors disappeared with it. Once again the kitchen was in shadowy darkness. This gray world, which had once been the only world he knew, now made Fredle sad, maybe because now he knew what he wasn't seeing.

"I'm worn out, aren't you?" Mister asked. "What a night."

"Exhausted," Missus agreed.

Behind his sadness, an idea was barking at Fredle, trying to get his attention. It barked and barked until at last he listened to what it wanted to tell him: *You can't wake up a baby that has been pushed out and left to went. You can't wake up something that isn't alive and asleep.*

Fredle was shocked. He was shocked and surprised and then he was so excited he thought he might bark, himself. The baby had been fixed and brought back home. Sadie had been right. Everything was all right, after all.

Without waiting any longer, he ran back to the mousehole behind the stove, and from there he climbed back up to his nest, his mind awhirl with a jumble of new ideas. The baby had been sick and the humans had kept it with them. They would keep it until it got better, whenever it was sick. Sadie had had a broken leg, like his grandmother, and a vet— whatever that was, it must be a human who fixed broken things—had fixed it for her. That was the way humans did things. Fredle didn't know *what* to think.

But when Fredle woke up the next evening, he knew just exactly what he thought. He thought: *Mice don't know everything.* He thought: *Some of the rules are wrong. OK, maybe not wrong so much as unnecessary. Not all the rules, and maybe not wrong for all mice, but definitely wrong for some.* That cheered him up. Another cheering thought was other creatures had some good ideas, and he already knew some of them.

Fredle needed cheering up because he was beginning to understand that with this living in light that was always gray and dim, with there being almost no color all around him all the time, and no stars, either, with rules that told you how you had to act even if you wanted to act differently, and with living among mice who were always so frightened and cautious that if you even *said* a mouse could act differently they would push you out—with all of these things . . . *What about with all these things?* he asked himself, but without any curiosity. He didn't want to know the answer to that question. These were uncomfortable and unhappy thoughts he was having. They made Fredle wish he didn't have to be a kitchen mouse, and what could he do about that?

What could he do, anyway, about anything? he wondered, but again without curiosity, since he already knew the answer, which was: *Nothing. What could any mouse do?* he asked himself hopelessly.

The answer to *that* question came, quickly and clearly, in his own voice from inside his own head, and Fredle barely had time to work out a plan before the nest began to wake up for the night.

The first mice he spoke to about the idea were his mother and father. He would have preferred to speak to all the kitchen mice at once, but unlike the cellar mice they didn't gather all together. It was too dangerous out in the kitchen and there was no room within the walls.

"Father?" Fredle began.

"Now what?"

"What if I were to go back outside? That's where I've been and you can see that I've survived, so what about if I did go back? And what if I took some mouselets with me? There's lots of room outside."

His territory behind the lattice would be a good place for mouselets to run around and play, and grow strong and healthy. They could make as much noise as they wanted to in the territory behind the lattice.

"Grandfather could come with me," Fredle added.

"Mice stay in the nests they were born in. You know that as well as I do, Fredle," Father said.

"And I'm about two and a half steps from went," Grandfather said. "What would be the point?"

Fredle ignored his father. He thought of Rilf and the Rowdy Boys and said to his grandfather, "You could see the moon, before. Wouldn't you rather have seen the moon, before you went?"

"If Fredle did that," said Mother, keeping her voice low, "he could take Ardle with him. And Doddle, too; Doddle has never been as healthy as a mouselet should be. And Kidle?" she suggested.

"Kidle is certainly headed for more trouble than I want to have to deal with," Father agreed. "Right now, all he does is talk. It's all talk, now, but you remember Fredle, what he was like at that age. And look at Fredle now," Father said. "He refuses to grow up and settle down."

"If Kidle wants to come with me, I'd like that," said Fredle.

"And any mouselets, too." He didn't give Father the time to say *I don't remember giving you permission*. "Tell them all to wait for me behind the stove when they've foraged. You, too, Grandfather. I promise, it's a long journey, and difficult, but not impossible, and if you come with me and if you see the moon—"

"I don't know that I can make it," Grandfather said.

"Just try," urged Fredle, and he slipped over the rim of the nest to go find Axle.

Axle, however, wasn't interested in moving to a new nest, especially a new nest outside. "Didn't you learn *anything* from what happened to us?" she asked. "Honestly, Fredle, don't you remember?"

He did. He remembered everything. The taste of chocolate and feeling sick, being alone and frightened, being near barn cats and snakes and raccoons, the way raptors fell out of the sky—of course he remembered. But he also remembered the look of those yellow flowers, their shining cups, and the way squirrels leapt through the grass in a burst of speed to run up the trunks of trees, and the taste of orange rind and the sound of chickens and what it was like to go out in the sunlight, if you wanted to, into a world full of color, or by moonlight into a world of silver shadows.

"Axle," he pleaded. "You'll like it. And besides, you could always come back here if you don't."

"I am quite happy here, now, where I am. Being grown-up."

"That's not the only way to be grown-up. I know one other and there are probably more than just those two."

"It's the only way *I* want to know, Fredle. So you can forget about dragging me around behind your wild ideas and I'm sorry that you can't see what's best for you."

"I'm sorry, too," Fredle said, but he didn't mean at all the same thing as Axle.

After that, he climbed down the walls into the kitchen. He didn't worry about foraging, because he knew that once he got to the cellar there would be plenty of food for everyone. And now that he thought of those baskets of food, he realized that with a nest behind the lattice, he could make piles of food, too, like the humans did, stores for the cold winter Neldo and Bardo had spoken of. Mice could carry food in their mouths, just like raccoons did, and pile up enough to feed them for a long time. He and the others might even move to the cellar when winter came, because if you could go from one nest to another, you could go from one to another to another. As he had said to Linu, *If you know the way to get there, then you also know the way back.*

Maybe Linu would want to come outside with him, and he and Neldo could show her flowers and squirrels and stars.

"Hello, Grandfather," he said as the old mouse came up to join him, with Kidle and four mouselets close behind.

"Here we are, then, young Fredle," Grandfather said. "What's next?"

Fredle told them, "We'll go down to the cellar, which isn't easy but we can do it, and then, after we have as much as we want to eat"—he could promise them that—"then we'll go up the cellar wall and across the dirt to outside."

"Will there be a moon?" Grandfather wondered.

"I don't know. It certainly could happen that one of the moons will be out in the sky."

"What's a moon?" asked Kidle.

"Or stars," Fredle said, remembering. "*And* stars."

"What's the sky?" asked Doddle.

"You'll see," Fredle told them. "You have no idea how much there is to see, and probably neither do I." He laughed with gladness, "Woo-Hah."

Later, much later, when things had turned out—sometimes as he'd planned, sometimes not as well as he'd wanted, and sometimes better than he'd hoped—Fredle told it like one of Grandfather's stories. He enjoyed it a great deal more in the

telling than he had in the living of it, or so he sometimes thought. And why should that be? he wondered, as he began, "When I was young, it was between the walls—inside—that was home."

As Fredle unfolded the story, there were certain points at which he was often interrupted: "But, Father, if she was too frightened to forage, why didn't your mother just eat from the stores?" "Aunt Linu, is that our same Sadie?" "Raccoons, Fredle? Did you hear that, Neldo? Fredle escaped from raccoons!" "What's a stove, Uncle Fredle?" "Did your grandfather get to see the moons? He did, didn't he?"

"I could never do what you did," they said, to which Fredle responded, "You'd be surprised at what you can do, if you need to, if you have to, if you really want to." However, there was always at least one of the mouselets who maintained, "I could, I could do it," and to him or her Fredle always said, "I know you could. I hope I'm around to see that."

And finally, after many seasons there came a mouselet who looked off up into the star-filled sky with dreaming eyes and repeated the word "Lake. Lake. Wouldn't you like to see a lake, Grandfather?"

Cynthia Voigt is the award-winning author of many books for young readers. Her accolades include a Newbery Medal for *Dicey's Song* (Book 2 in the Tillerman cycle), a Newbery Honor for *A Solitary Blue* (Book 3 in the Tillerman cycle), and the Margaret A. Edwards Award for Outstanding Literature for Young Adults. She is also the author of the Kingdom series, the Bad Girls series, and *Angus and Sadie*.

Cynthia Voigt lives with her husband in Maine. Please visit her on the Web at cynthiavoigt.com.

Louise Yates is the talented creator of two acclaimed picture books: *A Small Surprise* ("Will be sure to have readers in stitches." —*Kirkus Reviews*) and *Dog Loves Books* ("A gentle tale with a winning message." —*Publishers Weekly*, Starred).

She lives in London.

YEARLING ADVENTURE!

Looking for more great adventure books to read?
Check these out!

- ☐ *The Black Stallion and the Shape-shifter* by Steven Farley
- ☐ *The Broken Blade* by William Durbin
- ☐ *Century: Ring of Fire* by P. D. Baccalario
- ☐ *Danger on Midnight River* by Gary Paulsen
- ☐ *A Dog Called Grk* by Joshua Doder
- ☐ *Escape from Fire Mountain* by Gary Paulsen
- ☐ *Frozen Stiff* by Sherry Shahan
- ☐ *Leepike Ridge* by N. D. Wilson
- ☐ *Mr. Tucket* by Gary Paulsen
- ☐ *The Navigator* by Eoin McNamee
- ☐ *The Nine Pound Hammer* by John Claude Bemis
- ☐ *Oracles of Delphi Keep* by Victoria Laurie
- ☐ *The Phantom Tollbooth* by Norton Juster
- ☐ *Roland Wright: Future Knight* by Tony Davis
- ☐ *Space Bingo* by Tony Abbott
- ☐ *The Swiss Family Robinson* by Johann Wyss
- ☐ The Tapestry: *The Hound of Rowan* by Henry H. Neff
- ☐ *The Voyages of Doctor Dolittle* by Hugh Lofting
- ☐ *The Wolves of Willoughby Chase* by Joan Aiken
- ☐ *The Wreckers* by Iain Lawrence

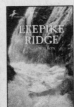

Visit **www.randomhouse.com/kids** for additional reading suggestions in fantasy, mystery, humor, and nonfiction!

Young Fredle
J FIC VOIGT   **31057011722843**

Voigt, Cynthia.
WEST GA REGIONAL LIBRARY SYS